# SCHRODINGER'S GOLD

# SCHRÖDINGER'S GOLD

## EMORY MOON

Published in the United States by Fowlbird Publishing
FowlBirdPublishing.com
Emory@fowlbirdpublishing.com

Fowl Bird Publishing and related logos are trademarks of Fowl Bird
Publishing

Some characters and events in this book are fictitious. Any similarity
to real persons, living or dead, is coincidental and not intended by
the author.

Library of Congress Cataloging-in-Publication Data is available
upon request

ISBN 979-8-9859992-2-8
First Edition

# TABLE OF CONTENTS

ACT 1

# SCHRODINGER'S GOLD

Moss hung from the oaks that lined the drive leading to the New Orleans, Garden District-adjacent home formerly known as Kensington Manor. Mrs. Kensington, widowed since 1900 when Mr. Kensington had died suddenly, remained in the only home she'd ever loved, seldom visited and lonely. Wild and various rumors of Mr. Kensington's untimely demise circulated through the local speakeasies and mercantile exchanges. Vile meanderings and subtle whisperings filled the air as folks speculated about his death. Some thought it was murder due to a business deal gone bad; others claimed it was related to witchcraft; some even suspected Mr. Kensington's wife. I gave the rumors no credence when I decided to co-habitat with Mrs. Kensington.

After being alone for many years and allowing the house to fall into disrepair, Mrs. Kensington had decided to open her doors for boarding purposes. Since I remain the only resident willing to speak on the matter, and since I was Mrs. Kensington's most dedicated and longstanding patron, I see it only befitting that I should relate to you the events leading to the dreadful downfall of her estate.

It was in the year 1929 that the boarding of various wanderers, vagabonds and strays began. Luckily, I was the first one who arrived at her door and, as such, was given special privileges often bestowed upon the first privy, such as first born, first love, and so on. I took it upon myself to exercise the rights given to me by choosing the second-best room in the house as my own, with the first-best reserved for the lady of the house. There we resided, Mrs. Kensington and I, for nearly fourteen months, without so much as a single solicitation for refuge. During this time, we developed a close and even kindred relationship. Mrs. Kensington indulged me, and we cherished the mutual company. However, from time to time, she did overstep the boundaries by volunteering the intricate details of her life and finances to my available ear. She often commented on my ability to listen to her tales without interruption, and I'm sure that was the reason for her biased favoritism toward me. By simply listening and offering my friendship to her, I learned the following things about The Kensingtons and their life and home.

She did not open her doors for financial gain but to battle the bitter loneliness accrued during her decades alone since the loss of Mr. Kensington. She had no children or other surviving family members. Both she and Mr. Kensington had resided in the Louisiana home since the completion of its construction in 1860. His father had given the home to the newlyweds as a gift. The manor was in the plantation style, in keeping with the era, and had been decorated to reflect this style. It sat upon fifty acres, rather small for a plantation of that period.

Mr. Kensington had not allowed overnight guests in his home and forbade boarders. On many occasions, he was known to have said, "There will be no pets allowed in this house of mine." Therefore, the idea was never entertained, even though Mrs. Kensington had voiced her desire for feline companionship many times. The staff kept the manor house in spotless order. Mr. Kensington adored his wife, on the one hand, but ruled over her, on the other, as was common in those days. Mrs. Kensington had been a loyal and doting companion to Mr. Kensington for the entirety of their forty-one years together, and she had complied with his every desire.

By 1931, Mrs. Kensington had gone entirely against his wishes and filled her home with a wide variety of patrons eager to stay in the twenty-seven-room mansion, ten of which were bedrooms. There were boarders from as far away as London, nine in total, including myself. Mr. and Mrs. O'Keefe were from St. Louis on vacation and had abandoned the idea of taking their train farther west, deciding to board with us instead. There were the two sisters, Kitty and Rose, from Alabama. Mrs. Kensington referred to Kitty as "Baby," even though she was the older of the two. The remaining five consisted of the following: one Leopold Standish, a short-haired British fellow who insisted upon wearing the same gray suit each and every day; Molly, a ragamuffin of a girl, who constantly boasted about her exotic fur, even though it was worn, tattered, and obviously not mink; Molly's friend Ginger, who wore a less fashionable patchwork coat, but one that I preferred, nevertheless; Josephine, as delicate as a ragdoll, with the deepest blue, most beautiful eyes I'd ever seen; and finally, me, Mr. Jasper Peabody, Mrs. Kensington's chosen favorite amongst all of her boarders, despite the difference in our ages.

There, we all resided at 113 Rue Cheshire, undisturbed for many, many months, engaging in extravagant caterings, performing mock balls, and getting along just famously. Twice weekly, Mrs. Kensington insisted upon dining in the grand dining hall. She made every attempt to suggest that the ordinary feast was actually a glamorous affair. In fact, on the eve prior, she would deliver to each room a gilded invitation that had been sealed with a crimson wax stamp, in which details of the impending event read:

`Greetings from 113 Rue Cheshire`
`The Kensingtons`
`do hereby request your presence at their home`
`for a formal gala to begin at 8:00 pm on`
`Sunday, December 10th, 1881`

--------------------------------------------------------------

-----------------------------

We gathered around the long mahogany table the next night to sup with Mrs. Kensington. She was a generous and fanciful hostess and made everyone feel at home, despite her handicap. She wheeled around the large table from place setting to place setting and insisted upon serving each meal without assistance. The fair was of staple quality, but I'm not one to complain, so I accepted my portion graciously and smiled at Mrs. Kensington. As expected, the O'Keefes were the best dressed, with Mr. O'Keefe donning an elegant black tuxedo. Mrs. O'Keefe had a complimenting black dress with white stockings. Both Josephine and Ginger wore their best attire, and when no one mentioned Molly's coat upon her entrance, she was taken aback and acted miffed for the remainder of the evening. Other than that, the night was a fun-filled time, enjoyed by all.

"Do you like your meal, Sugar?" Mrs. Kensington asked as she bestowed a term of endearment upon Josey.

"Are the rest of you ladies getting along well?" she inquired as she looked at Baby, and then at Rose.

"How is yours, Mr. Peabody?"

I gave an approving nod and continued eating.

After dinner, Mrs. Kensington suggested that we all retire to the "theater." There, she wound the Victrola, placed the needle upon the rotating surface, and the sound of sad, sweet music filled the room as we all moved about and mingled quietly. The "library," as I called it, was lined with judge's paneling and wainscoting, with shelves and shelves of books from ceiling to floor. An old, black, cast-iron ladder on rollers sat in the far corner but remained attached to the bookshelves. Mrs. Kensington referred to this room as the "theater," even though it was, in fact, a library. It was furnished in the Victorian style with fancy, wooden, wing-back chairs highlighted with deep, rich, velveteen fabrics, leather sofas and ottomans accented with brass tack after brass tack, and one fringed, Oriental rug covering the entire floor. The chandelier that once hung in the center of the room had long since vanished, due to the financial burdens that Mrs. Kensington had often faced since being widowed. These troublesome times did not seem to bother Mrs. Kensington and she continued to indulge her guests twice weekly.

We adjourned to the balcony just off the library for a nightcap after the musical interlude, and Mrs. Kensington, being somewhat reflective, engaged me with a proposition.

## **The Proposition**

"Dear Mr. Peabody," she said, "if only you were up to governing my home once I am gone."

I said nothing in response, and Mrs. Kensington did not remark on my silence. I had heard this all before, at almost every cotillion since I had arrived at her door. It was always the same—the same tone, the same urgency, the same subtlety. "Dear Mr. Peabody, if only you were up to governing my home once I am gone." But she always left it at that and had not yet asked me outright.

This may be a presumption on my part here, but I felt like Mrs. Kensington's repeated attempts to employ me were her way of suggesting that I begin the job immediately. Why shouldn't I take charge of the home? With the proper assistance, I could run the house as well as Mrs. Kensington herself. I would make a fine host for the bi-weekly events, and I already had previous experience.

So I took it upon myself to see to it that Mrs. Kensington was not disappointed, and I, reluctantly, at first, agreed to abide by her wishes.

## The Promotion

The following night, I called a boarders' meeting, and we all congregated in the gallery on the third floor to discuss my new duties as envoy and co-host for Kensington Manor. I was congratulated and showered with many compliments as I made each patron aware of my promotion within the house. There, we lingered for several hours under celebratory regalia, and news of my good fortune was the primary topic of conversation. Then, after finding no suggestions in the suggestion box, which was normally processed as first-order-of-business, I extended my sincere gratitude for my boarding mates' support and returned to my room. Attached to the knob of my chamber door via a tassel in royal blue was the ever-so-familiar invitation.

And as usual, it read:

```
        Greetings from 113 Rue Cheshire
              The Kensingtons
  do hereby request your presence at their home
    for a formal gala to begin at 8:00 pm on
         Sunday, December 10th, 1881
------------------------------------------------------

        ----------------------------
```

Mrs. Kensington served each patron as we sat at our usual places along the large dining table. She did not seem to be herself and acted befuddled and nervous. I wondered about the reason for the variation in having two nearly consecutive galas, but I never questioned the lady of the house, and therefore, remained mum on the subject. After all, I certainly had nothing to complain about and nowhere better to be. After dinner, we retired to the "theater" where, as usual, Mrs. Kensington readied the Victrola.

## The Predicament

"May I speak to you in private, Mr. Peabody?" she asked me once the music began.

We moved from the library onto the balcony, and Mrs. Kensington closed the French doors behind us. Now that Mrs. Kensington had obtained my reluctant agreement to assist in affairs of her estate, and now that I had begun the action plan to enact her wishes, it seemed that Mrs. Kensington was having second thoughts regarding the entire affair. She went on to tell me about how Mr. Kensington had begun visiting her in the night. She relayed this information to me in a giddy schoolgirl-type of fashion, and she seemed to be under the impression they were courting.

"Mr. Peabody, I'm afraid we've upset Mr. Kensington," she said. "He's very angry with me. I'm afraid I must ask you and all the others to vacate the premises."

I could not believe the words just spoken by my hostess.

"Since you are the elder statesman here, will you please convey my desires to the others?" she asked. "Thank you, Mr. Peabody," she added before I could reply. And with that, she opened the French doors and wheeled from the balcony into the library and through to the hallway on the other side.

Since all the boarders had taken notice of Mrs. Kensington's abrupt departure, they stared upon my speechless face as the Victrola came to a distorted halt. I remained unable to address them as I felt their uneasiness grow.

## The Plan

The boarders' meeting was called to order as I presided over the commencement. And once again, after finding no suggestions within the suggestion box, I relayed Mrs. Kensington's message to the entire congregation and waited for their reaction. It was mutually agreed that we should employ every method possible to convince Mrs. Kensington to abandon her plan of eviction. But how?

It was decided that we should go about business as usual, in hopes that Mrs. Kensington might forget her preposterous demand and refrain from evicting us from the estate. So, the next day, we did just that. I woke early, as usual, and wandered down the stairs. As I descended the grand staircase, I could hear Mrs. Kensington speaking to a yet-unknown third party.

"Can you help me?" she asked through the manor's partially opened front door. The response was muffled and incoherent to my otherwise sharp ears. "I have asked them to vacate my home, but here they remain," Mrs. Kensington continued. Upon seeing my approach, Mrs. Kensington changed her tone and quickly bade farewell to the anonymous visitor.

I stood motionless at the base of the stairs and stared at Mrs. Kensington as she exited the foyer, rolled into the dining hall and up to the fireplace, removed a feather duster from the pouch tied to the side of her wheelchair, and began dusting the mantle.

## The Portrait

"There, there, Mr. Kensington... Things will be back to normal soon," she said as she continued to tend the mantle with the duster. Just above the mantel, on the wall, hung a huge, framed oil portrait of a young Mr. Kensington, armed and uniformed. Immediately behind that was a safe, unopened since long before the widowing, and just below the painting, an elaborate, glazed, clay urn which had been turned by Mrs. Kensington on her pottery wheel and designated as her future resting place for all eternity. Mrs. Kensington continued to dust the painting as she now spoke to me.

"I thought you would be gone by now, Mr. Peabody," she said as she continued her work. "Mr. Kensington has been very patient with all of us."

I said nothing. After all, how do you respond to an old lady who is simply off-her-rocker, as they say?

"You all have until the weekend to vacate, Mr. Peabody," she said as she rolled off toward the kitchen.

-------------------------------------------------------

-----------------------------

Several months later, Mrs. Kensington had not forgotten. She continued the strange, standoffish behavior, and there were no more elaborate galas. On numerous occasions, she solicited help from various callers to her door.

## **The Plea**

"Please, you must help me," she implored.

Mr. Bainbridge, the weekly courier, sat upon the French provincial sofa sipping a cup of tea as Mrs. Kensington pleaded her case.

"They have refused to leave my home and have threatened to harm Mr. Kensington and me if the matter is pursued," she continued.

"Mrs. Kensington." Mr. Bainbridge paused. "Mr. Kensington is no longer with us. I'm sure he would not mind you having company at this stage in your life."

"He does mind. He told me so himself," she replied.

"I really think it's okay for you to have them here. You mustn't continue to fret about this so," Mr. Bainbridge said in an attempt to reassure her.

I continued to watch from the upper landing as Mrs. Kensington continued to plead her case. After their brief conversation, I determined the result of her pleas to be inconclusive. I never heard Mr. Bainbridge accept or reject Mrs. Kensington's S.O.S. outright.

## The Proclamation

Mr. Kensington had been a wealthy man, born to a wealthy family. His father and his father's father were also the wealthiest of men, in charge of Kensington Plantation since its inception many years prior to the American Revolution.

In 1863, upon President Lincoln's enactment of the Emancipation Proclamation, the Kensington estate fell into decline, thus giving birth to Kensington's Treasure. Rumor had it, during his occasional furloughs Mr. Kensington had begun to hoard, at first, one valuable, then another. His fear, fed by the continued faltering of his plantation, weighed heavily on his mind, and therefore, his hoarding increased. He began by selling off the various framed oils, sculptures and adornments that filled the manor house, including the masterpiece, *The Headless Horseman Pursuing Ichabod Crane, 1858.* He liquidated almost everything, thus converting the works of art to gold, then stowing that away for safekeeping. This selling and hoarding were well-documented at the time. However, the net result of his behavior remained in doubt. Some say he lost it at the card tables, while others claimed it was buried there on the plantation grounds, but the consensus of those questioned was that it remained there, somewhere inside the manor house.

Furthermore, it was rumored that the Wells Fargo safe behind the portrait that hung on the wall just above the mantle in the grand dining hall in the manor house on the Kensington estate held a hefty but undetermined fortune, primarily in gold. Unfortunately, the safe had not been opened, to anyone's knowledge, since the passing of Mr. Kensington, and from stories I heard, much longer than that. You see, the combination had been inscribed inside the hunter's case of Mr. Kensington's inherited gold watch, which was lost and had long since been forgotten due to the failure to record the numbers in any secondary location. As the years passed, and as the gossip and rumors continued to build, it was suggested, via this chatter, that the fortune in question may or may not reside within the security of the iron box behind the portrait that hung on the wall just above the mantle. After all, there was some doubt regarding the treasure, and there was, in fact, no 'proof' of its existence, at all.

Additionally, the rumors regarding Mr. Kensington's involvement in the 'Confederate Gold' scandal propelled this scuttlebutt into legend and, if true, would make Kensington Manor the most valuable estate in all the nation. As a result, based upon this hearsay and doubt, a curiosity regarding Kensington's treasure evolved into the mystery we know today as Schrodinger's Gold. In short, the riches 'may' or 'may not' remain housed within the safe behind the portrait that hangs on the wall just above the mantle in the grand dining hall of the manor house on the Kensington estate. This curiosity was the catalyst for my investigation.

## The Power of Attorney

Who authorized me to conduct this investigation? Well, no one. I mean, there was no power-of-attorney or any other formal document permitting me to investigate. Let's just say, my curiosity forced me, especially after my hostess had shared numerous falsehoods on the subjects of Mr. Kensington and Kensington Manor. Had this misinformation related only to one prior event, I might have overlooked it, but the longer I resided at Kensington Manor, the more discrepancies I discovered. These discoveries split my investigation in two. One leg of my investigation was in search of the truth as it pertained to Mr. Kensington's death and Schrodinger's Gold. The other was to find out why Mrs. Kensington's behavior toward us boarders abruptly changed.

## The Presentation

Therefore, based upon my aforementioned curiosity, piqued by the suspicious documents found in Mr. Kensington's desk, I present to you the following full accounting of the events, witnesses, and suspects, as investigated by yours truly, Mr. Jasper Peabody.

ACT 2

# 113 RUE CHESHIRE

**<u>The Plantation</u>**

One-thirteen Rue Cheshire sat back, some 300 yards from the main road. The wrought iron gates that separated the estate from the Garden District and New Orleans proper had been forged by Mr. Kensington during better times when the bellows of the onsite livery and blacksmith shop still had reason to blow. Towering oaks lined both sides of the drive that led from the gates to the main house, and they—the trees and the gates—were now the only aesthetics to remain as they had once been.

Flowers no longer bloomed on the grounds in the spring or the summer.

There were no rows of crops to provide vegetables or orchards to bear fruit. The formerly congruent brick fence with whitewashed rails was now broken and unsound, rendering it unfit to contain the heads of livestock that had once roamed the grounds. Pothole after pothole appeared now, where cobblestones had formerly laid, making it impossible for poor Mrs. Kensington to truly enjoy the outdoors. And no matter how intently you might listen, even

13

by remaining completely motionless, reducing the twigs beneath your feet to utter silence, there was not a single 'cluck' to be heard from hen or rooster. The once pristine estate had become derelict and overgrown since the widowing of Mrs. Kensington. I found nothing of value there except for the one travertine bird bath in the overgrown courtyard between the main house and the servants' quarters. The neglected bath was dirty and filled with dead leaves, so it remained devoid of both aqua and Aves. This is how I found the grounds of 113 Rue Cheshire on the date of my arrival.

## The Particulars

The dwelling at 113 Rue Cheshire, my domicile to this day, was in slightly better order on the inside than on the outside. The once white exterior was now worn and faded, and in the areas where it was not worn and faded, the paint was absent altogether, the chips lying undisturbed where they'd fallen over the years. The two-story white columns were also aged well beyond their purpose, which would most likely relegate them into a class of condemnation if subjected to inspection. Inside, the electric lights no longer illuminated, whether by day or by night, and the chandelier in the foyer was absent altogether. I found the wine cellar devoid of even one bottle; that is to say, even one bottle that contained wine. Most of the oil paintings, and all the tapestries and sculptures, were no longer present, with the exception of the one oil painting that remained above the fireplace. The silver utensils, candlesticks, and snuffers were also missing. The only room left undisturbed from the manor's decline was the study where Mr. Kensington had conducted manor business.

## The Pocket Watch

Inspection of Mr. Kensington's study produced the following. I located a private journal in the top drawer of his desk. Daily entries had been made that went well beyond the date of his death. The diary also contained a full inventory of the valuables once housed in his Manor home, along with dates and dollar amounts, implying they had been sold at some point. Many documents and letters, both stamped and unstamped, were found. Further investigation suggested that his elaborate pipe collection was not present. Nor were his prized possessions and family heirlooms—specifically, his gold pocket watch and fob, once owned by his father's father. This is how I found the contents of the estate at 113 Rue Cheshire on the day I arrived.

## The Perusal

After accepting my promotion as the envoy of Kensington Manor, I decided the timing was right to launch my investigations into the unsettling events that contributed to the downfall of Kensington Manor. I began by examining the journal I'd found in Mr. Kensington's desk. It was a wealth of knowledge, and from it, I gained much insight into the history of Kensington Manor and the tragedy that occurred prior to my arrival.

## The Pianist

The Kensingtons, at one time, had employed many staff and servants who fulfilled every need and desire placed before them. They lived a life of leisure and over-indulgence, a life to which most of us can only aspire. The galas and cotillions were extravagant, the next always grander than the last. I've learned of a bitter feud that arose between Mrs. Kensington and a pianist commissioned to be in attendance to provide entertainment during the many extravaganzas. I'm told this disagreement originated during the last formal gathering just before Mr. Kensington's death. Could this have been a motive to kill him? I suppose it could.

## <u>The Pauper</u>

Not long after this final soiree, as Mrs. Kensington made her departure from the wake to celebrate her life with Mr. Kensington, she was approached in the street by an individual unknown to her who claimed to have exclusive knowledge related to Mr. Kensington's death. This self-proclaimed witness was written off as an opportunist at the time, based upon their state of inebriation, and based upon their ragged appearance, suggesting they were outwardly destitute and in need of money, making them suspicious for blackmail or bribery.

## <u>The Plumber</u>

That same evening, upon her return to the manor house, Mrs. Kensington found her home in disarray. The staff informed her of a water leak originating in the basement. The lower level of the home, including the wine cellar, the walk-in humidor, the cold storage, the gymnasium, and the cannery, now stood nearly six inches deep in water. A tradesman from the pipefitter's local union was already on the scene and hard at work attempting to halt the flow of water.

## <u>The Physician</u>

The stress of this calamity, coupled with the recent loss of her husband, proved more than Mrs. Kensington could bear, resulting in an immediate loss of consciousness and a laceration upon her forehead due to the subsequent fall from her wheelchair. A note to Mrs. Kensington's private physician, Dr. Condos Poirot was dispatched immediately. He arrived at her bedside within the hour, where he diagnosed her condition as grave.

## The Preacher

Mrs. Kensington's clergyman and lifelong friend was summoned in expectation of the worst, and there he remained, along with the doctor, throughout this tumultuous time.

## The Prayer

As her condition worsened, less than twenty-four hours after Mr. Kensington's burial, the clergyman recited the Lord's Prayer in accordance with Mrs. Kensington's religious beliefs.

## The Parsonage

One week later, as Mrs. Kensington's condition improved, the Southern Baptist preacher returned to his parsonage with his overnight bag in one hand and his Bible in the other.

## The Prescription

To enhance Mrs. Kensington's improvement, her doctor prescribed medication to hasten her recovery.

## The Poinsettia

The day after Mrs. Kensington awakened, a florist delivered a single potted Poinsettia adorned with numerous bright red blooms. A straight pin fastened a sealed card to the golden-silver foil that adorned the pot. Mrs. Kensington removed the card and read it silently before tucking it into the pocket of the apron she wore daily, by choice, and not by necessity.

## The Pachyderm

Two days later, Mrs. Kensington was up and about, tending to her chores just as before. Her faculties were now fully restored, and she rolled about the house 'piddling,' as she called it, with the only noticeable change to her behavior being this—she no longer dusted and talked to the portrait that hung above the mantle in the grand dining hall, as she'd done daily before her accident. Instead, around sunset every evening, she began to dust and talk to the mounted head of the bull Rhinoceros that hung in Mr. Kensington's study—the very head of the formerly-living pachyderm killed by Mr. Kensington himself while on safari. This behavior, while odd, wasn't enough for Mrs. Kensington's commitment to any mental institution, but rather, indicative of her continued decline.

## The Parable

At the base of the head, inscribed upon the plate attached to the mount, it read: *If I don't kill that Rhino, somebody else will.* Over the years, I heard Mrs. Kensington recite these words often. I never ascribed any significance to the verse.

The head and the portrait were the only two decorative items to survive the decline of Kensington Manor. I later learned of another mount owned by Mr. Kensington, which he had valued even more than his watch or his rhino.

## The Palomino

A thoroughbred horse once graced the plantation, loping and galloping at will, with his mane flowing majestically in the wind behind him. Mr. Kensington had taken solace in watching the magnificent beast of burden as he roamed about the green rolling hills. Most evenings, Mr. Kensington could be found standing just outside the fence, watching his prized mount until the fireflies saturated the night. In short, Mr. Kensington loved this horse.

After many years spent in awe of the animal, Mr. Kensington experienced an abrupt change in attitude toward his friend. The Palomino, without explanation, was sold at auction and never mentioned again. One theory suggests the proceeds from this transaction are, in fact, a portion of Schrodinger's Gold, while a second theory suggests something entirely different.

## The Phantom

Present that day at auction was a mysterious man unknown to all the other attendees. Some interviewees suggested this man might be a former associate of Mr. Kensington, maybe even a fellow soldier and member of the same regiment of Pointe Coupee, organized under Colonel Richard Atlantic Stewart who, at the time, was only a captain. Further probing uncovered a certain discord and dissent within the regiment, described as follows:

## Pointe Coupee

In late 1861, Mr. Kensington, along with many other young men of New Orleans, was recruited into the Pointe Coupee regiment and sent for artillery training at Baton Rouge, where they were instructed on and equipped with the finest ordnance available at that time. Subsequently, Mr. Kensington and his regiment engaged the enemy at Island Number Ten on the Mississippi, Vicksburg, the Second Battle of Corinth, numerous other battles, and later, at Port Hudson, Louisiana.

## The Philippi Races

At the very beginning of the American Civil War, at what was the very first organized land engagement between North and South, before Mr. Kensington had been recruited into the artillery, he and several other members of his regiment, had participated in the Battle of Philippi. This Union victory was attributed to Mr. Kensington's regiment's lack of training and lack of battle readiness and can be better described as a forfeiture due to the mass retreat of Southern troops. This retreat, laughingly referred to as the 'Philippi Races' by Union soldiers, was reported to be the central issue giving birth to the discord amongst Mr. Kensington and his comrades. As the southerners fled west from Virginia during the skirmish, the matter of loyalty arose among the Confederates, resulting in disagreement and infighting. This matter of loyalty was never determined; to this day, no one knows who remained or who retreated. Furthermore, the aforementioned phantom's identity could have been any one of his former comrades participating in the races that day.

## The Partisan Ranger Act

The Partisan Ranger Act of the Confederate States of America was adopted in April 1862 in an attempt to increase the number of active duty ranks for the Confederacy. This congressional act was intended to formalize the many bands of already-existing Confederate guerrilla fighters into more controlled and coordinated regiments. Later, in August of 1862, this act formalized the commission of William Quantrill of Missouri to organize his own regiment, giving birth to Quantrill's Raiders, otherwise known as the Bushwhackers.

The Bushwhackers, bitter and vengeful against the North, often acted outside the law by killing civilians, including women and children. These acts placed black marks against the names of each member of Quantrill's Regiment, officially designating them as outlaws and desperados. It was at this time that Quantrill's Raiders and the Artillery Regiment of Pointe Coupee saw action together for the first time as allied armies at the First Battle of Independence in Jackson County, Missouri. It was also here that the newly trained artilleryman, Private Kensington, would cross paths and fight alongside the notorious James brothers and Younger brothers, future founders of the James-Younger Gang, and current members of Quantrill's Raiders.

The Confederate victory at the First Battle of Independence was due, in part, to the particularly barbaric offensives led by the Bushwhackers.

Just a few days later, the Confederacy and the Bushwhackers were at it again, fighting against Union Major Emory Foster and his men at the Battle of Lone Jack. Union troops suffered heavy losses during this one-day skirmish, which reduced their presence at Lone Jack by nearly fifty percent, costing them approximately 400 men. The desperado guerilla tactics of the South seemed like a recipe for victory.

Nearly one year later, after Quantrill and his men had laid low for the winter, they engaged the enemy again in Lawrence, Kansas, elevating their barbarity even higher. When a skirmish or fight earns the moniker of 'massacre' over 'battle,' then we have to ask ourselves: To what depths can the inhumanity of men sink?

The Lawrence Massacre of August 21, 1863 left 164 civilians dead, mostly unarmed men and boys. This attack, perpetrated by the Bushwhackers against the Jayhawkers, also known as (aka) The Redlegs, another vigilante group, was a heinous act driven by revenge, in retaliation for the continued Jayhawk support for the North. The massacre was condemned by Confederate leaders.

The Baxter Springs Massacre followed, with almost equal brutality, in October 1863, when Quantrill and his men ambushed Union troops near Baxter Springs. By this time, and with no further recourse to reign in the brutality of the Bushwhackers, the Confederate States of America withdrew all backing formerly given to Quantrill's Raiders, including financial and tactical support.

By winter of 1863, Quantrill had lost all authority within his regiment, resulting in their dissolution and disbursement throughout the south and west, where some of them would eventually reunite as outlaws of the Old West.

## Port Hudson

Mr. Kensington and his fellow confederates, now under General Pierre G.T. Beauregard, were ordered to 'fortify' Port Hudson, and thus, arrived in the port in August of 1862, whence the fortification began. The bluffs along the banks of the river at the port were well-suited for defending the area, and before long, but after some debate on the particulars, the fortification was complete. The Union Army responded to this build-up along the Mississippi with the steam-powered USS Essex, which began a bombardment of the port in September. This initial attack on the port resulted in heavy damage to the Essex, and thus began a protracted engagement between North and South over control of the port. Both Mr. Kensington and the 'unnamed phantom' performed well during this time. However, their mutual discord, which originated during the races, remained.

## The Plains Store Battle

In early May of 1863, as Union Troops advanced toward the Louisiana stronghold of Port Hudson, it became imperative to the South that this advancement be halted. Unfortunately, the Battle of Plains Store on May 21st, a Union victory, forced the Confederates to retreat into Port Hudson, reducing chances of escape.

## The Plantation Battle of Stirling

The once energetic, shrewd, and decisive Private Kensington was now battle-fatigued and despondent. He had performed well in all prior campaigns, but while under the constant onslaught from the enemy, he began to question his role within his regiment and within the American Civil War, as a whole. While only holding the rank of private, an oversight on his army's behalf, his natural abilities to improvise strategies, based upon his uncanny insight into enemy troop deployments and movements, heightened his worry. Based on this insight, he became concerned about an imminent Confederate surrender. During his final Battle with the Confederacy at Stirling's Plantation, a Confederate victory, Private Kensington, while under this aforementioned duress, made his final war-related decision.

On September 29, 1863, amidst the pandemonium and chaos that raged that day during the battle, the Confederates captured 454 enemy soldiers, along with all of their weapons and some much-needed medical supplies, while only losing thirty-six men in return, with twenty-six of those being killed and the other ten missing. When a roll call was taken afterward, Private Kensington was marked within the ledger as 'missing.'

## The Paranoia

Mr. Kensington's decision that day was not an easy one. By this time, his growing fear of capture or death, or both, consumed his every waking moment. Overwhelmed by these paranoid thoughts, coupled with his burning desire to see his Manor home one more time, he acted.

## The Proximity

The continued fighting had brought Mr. Kensington to within 100 miles of his beloved Kensington Manor and as his imagination ran wild, thoughts of Union occupation of his former home became unbearable.

## Parlange, LA

As he began to make his way south toward New Orleans in the darkness of night, a powerful disorientation, most likely due to battle fatigue and the fever he had contracted, redirected him in a northerly direction, resulting in his displacement to Parlange, Louisiana.

## The Pumpkin Patch

Arriving in Parlange disoriented, feverish, and malnourished, Mr. Kensington collapsed in the midst of a tremendous pumpkin patch bordering a plantation that dwarfed his own. There, he lay for nearly forty-eight hours until discovered by slaves working nearby.

Nearly a week elapsed before Mr. Kensington awakened within a cramped crawl space in the servants' quarters of Yvonne and her younger sister on Fontaineaux Plantation in Parlange.

## The Poultice

A vinegar-based poultice of onion, to reduce fever, had been placed upon his forehead and wrapped around his feet, and while his fever had been reduced, the disorientation remained. He talked nonsense, believing he was still on the battlefield, and speaking of treasures and other outlandish things. His caretakers, slaves of the Fontaineauxs, thought nothing of his ramblings or his wartime affiliation when they began to nurse him back into good health.

Nearly a week later, Mr. Kensington regained his composure and asked his nursemaid to advise him on both Union troops and Confederate troops in the area. She obliged and informed him regarding both, explaining to him that parties from both the North and the South had been to her door and searched her quarters for deserters. She suggested that he continue to hide beneath the floorboards of her cabin, just beneath her boiling pot, where he could remain unseen from both the interior and exterior of her dwelling.

Taking her suggestion, Mr. Kensington remained with her periodically taking refuge beneath the floorboards to evade capture.

Three months later, he made his way west on the back of a wayward horse whose rider had been killed in battle nearby.

ACT 3

# JAMES YOUNGER KENSINGTON

**<u>The Pistoleros</u>**

Many western outlaws and gunfighters were born in the years following the American Civil War. This upheaval during America's history gave birth to a colorful and mysterious period in time known as the Old West. Men marked as deserters became outlaws as they moved westward in search of wealth and freedom. The ones well-trained in self-defense and action with their sidearms usually acquired more wealth but in exchange, lost their freedom. Mr. Kensington, along with an unknown number of his comrades, would suffer this fate, resulting in many years of estrangement from their families and homes. Mr. Kensington ultimately returned to New Orleans after the war but did not arrive there until December of 1881.

**<u>The Parlay</u>**

In uncertain times, men make choices that go against the grain of their souls. Facing an unknown future, possible imprisonment, or death can reduce some men to behave in previously unthinkable ways. This was, indeed, my assessment of the following event that changed the opinion of Mr. Kensington in the eyes of many and resulted in a net increase of enemies toward him. Mr. Kensington, once an outright wealthy and gentle man, was changed by the horrors of war. His once optimistic outlook on life died on the battlefields, where he routinely witnessed, first-hand, amputation and death. With his spirit now broken, and sensing his limited time on this earth, coupled with his fear of surrendering his inheritance to the North, he made his decision to gamble on his future.

## The Ponzi

Approximately six months before Mr. Kensington's desertion, he and at least three others, but possibly five, developed an intricate scheme to defraud the Confederate States of America by manipulating the payroll data periodically reported to their government. Over time, these men collected thousands of dollars in the names of dead Confederate soldiers, thus pocketing these funds for personal gain. I suspect only one other man as a co-conspirator in this fraud, as my investigation is ongoing. To identify him by name without evidence would be unprofessional.

## The Pay Master

It wasn't all that long before government agents began to notice the discrepancy between the deaths reported and the payroll. In the months when regiments reported a deflation within their ranks due to deaths outpacing new recruits, the payroll would naturally follow suit, reflecting a decline in payroll. The opposite would prove true when regiments gained manpower. Therefore, the key element required to perpetuate this payroll ruse was to make sure that payroll data maintained pace with active soldier data, no matter the validity of the data. Theoretically, the gap between the payroll and active duty men should always follow the same up, then down, then up, then down, trajectory. The failure to maintain this rhythm was their undoing, and before long, the origins of this scam were being investigated by agents of the Confederacy.

## The Pariah

James Younger Kensington was not his name, but rather, his affiliation. I suppose you've heard of the James-Younger Gang, headed by those ruthless outlaws Jesse and Frank James and Bob and Cole Younger. Well, had history unfolded in a slightly different way, the James-Younger Gang could have been known as the James-Younger-Kensington Gang, or possibly, the Kensington-James-Younger Gang.

During the days of the Old West, and as gangs of outlaws formed and disbanded and then reformed again, the membership or affiliation of these gangs fluctuated with each new iteration. Each of the men listed below have been known to belong to the James-Younger Gang, within one of those iterations, and in some instances, more than one. Obviously, the long-term members Jesse and Frank James were founders, and members from beginning to end, as were the Youngers, Bob and Cole, but at varying times. The membership also included: Jim and John Younger, Arthur McCoy, George and Oliver Shepherd, William and Tom McDaniel, Clell Miller, Charlie Pitts, Tucker Basham, Bill Chadwell, aka Bill Stiles, Thorogood "Bull" Kensington, Bob and Charles Ford, and several other unnamed individuals who either betrayed other members of the gang or whose role within the gang was so insignificant that history has not seen fit to mention them. This insignificance could account for the gang's moniker, but as I've learned, the role of Mr. Thorogood Kensington was not insignificant, at all.

## The Permutation

Many men traverse their time here on earth with no defining events occurring within their lives. Their time waxes, then wanes, without them ever experiencing an event that alters their course in history. If ever a defining point occurred within the life of Mr. Thorogood "Bull" Kensington, it must have been the following.

After Mr. Kensington allegedly acquired and then locked away some of his fortune at Kensington Manor, after he engraved the combination into the case of his gold watch, and after his conscription into the Army of the Confederate States of America, a bit of bad luck began to infiltrate his life.

During his very first engagement with Union troops at the Battle of Philipi, and during the mass exodus of Confederate troops that occurred afterward, Mr. Kensington's irreplaceable watch fell into the hands of the North and was declared, 'spoils of war.' This singular event enraged T. 'Bull' Kensington and altered the course of his life and time in history. His only dream was to return to Kensington Manor to resume the life he'd once known. His only thought, a thought that consumed him daily, was of the watch and its return to its rightful owner, and as the months passed, a certain measure and desire for revenge began to change him. He no longer behaved in his formerly kind and sophisticated manner. In short, he became an outlaw.

## The Parish-Bienville Stagecoach - 1874

Years after Mr. Kensington had abandoned his post and his comrades and headed west, and years after allowing the revenge to swell within him, an unexpected event, once again, altered his trajectory in life. Mr. Kensington had heard a tale of a certain gold watch captured by the Union in which there had been inscribed what was presumed to be a safe's combination. This watch had been recovered from a Union officer as his body lay dead upon the battlefield. This watch provided no information regarding the location of the safe, thus rendering the combination that it held useless to most.

In deciding to follow the gossip, Mr. Kensington found himself in the Louisiana Parish of Bienville in 1874, some 300 miles from his hometown, where he lay in wait for a southbound stagecoach. Just as he began to act, the coach came under attack from a group he did not immediately recognize. The stagecoach was halted and robbed. No one on the coach that day possessed the watch. During the commotion, Mr. Kensington was recognized by the thieves as their former Confederate comrade, prompting an invitation to join them. He readily accepted and left there with the bandits as they galloped away.

This was Mr. Kensington's introduction to the James-Younger Gang. Afterward, once Mr. Kensington and the thieves were well away from the scene of the crime and holed up within a safehouse, Mr. Kensington relayed his mutual intent regarding the robbery. He told the gang of his beloved and inherited watch and how it had fallen prey to the North. This mutual hatred for the Union solidified his position within the gang. It wasn't long before Mr. Kensington and his fellow gang members were at it again.

## Price, Arkansas - 1874

Later that same year, approximately halfway between Hot Springs and Malvern, Arkansas, the gang robbed another stagecoach. Onboard and in possession of a particular gold watch, one of the travelers, a northern gentleman headed for Hot Springs, was relieved of all his immediate wealth. It was decided unanimously amongst the Jameses and the Youngers that this watch should be returned to its rightful owner, and based upon the description given to them earlier by Mr. Kensington, there was no doubt regarding his identity. Therefore, in gratitude for his service on behalf of the Confederate States of America, and as a symbol of perceived victory over the North, the gold watch was presented to Mr. Kensington, and further solidified his bond within this brotherhood of outlaws.

## The Pacific Railroad - December 1874

The first train robbery after Mr. Kensington's induction into the James-Younger Gang would prove to be the most lucrative to date. On December 8th, 1874, in Muncie, Kansas, the Kansas leg of the Pacific Railroad was robbed of an estimated thirty thousand dollars, and while this particular robbery proved financially beneficial, it was not without its costs. One member of the gang was captured and then shot dead while attempting to escape.

## The Press

It was at this time, a rival gang headed up by Arthur McCoy also began to gain notoriety for their lawlessness. The similarities between the two gangs often led to discrepancies in eyewitness testimonies. The robbery of the Iron Mountain Railway in Missouri was just one of the crimes attributed to the incorrect criminals. This misidentification infuriated Jesse James, forcing him to seek immediate and public clarification. So, after the robbery and after the newspapers had printed the facts of the case, as reported to them, Thorogood Kensington, on direct orders from Jesse, wired the St. Louis Dispatch demanding a retraction, telegraphing them the facts regarding the robbery and supplying the correct attributions.

## The Perpetrators

As the years rolled by, and as the gang-related crimes and atrocities continued, the identity of each gang member involved became widely known, with each man's name, and sometimes his photograph, landing on the front pages of the nation's many newspapers and chronicles. Some of the gang members who'd played only minor roles in the crimes were never mentioned, and over time, forgotten. Other participants kept their names out of print via aliases and nicknames. This happened to be the case for Thorogood 'Bull' Kensington. Legend has it that upon their first meeting Jesse James said, "And you are?"

And Thorogood Kensington simply replied, "The Bull."

Legend also states that this commanding response from Kensington to James was met with respect and admiration, since few men spoke to Jesse in that way, and 'The Bull' became a highly regarded confidant of the infamous gang leader. Mr. Kensington spent the entirety of his gang affiliation being addressed and referred to as just 'Bull' or 'The Bull.' None of them ever knew his real name.

## The Persuasion

In 1874, Silas Woodson, Governor of Missouri offered an official government persuasion to the public. Reward money, in the amount of two thousand dollars, was offered for the Iron Mountain robbers. This amount was substantially higher than usual. Woodson also secured funding to cover expenses for the tracking and the apprehension of the criminals. This government-backed directive almost guaranteed the capture of members of the James-Younger Gang.

## The Pistol

News of the reward shook Jesse and the others but did not slow the pace of their crimes. Instead, the audacity of their criminal enterprise seemed to use such reports as fodder for their brazenness.

In 1875, just after losing several more members of their syndicate, it was rumored that Jesse James gave 'The Bull' an engraved sidearm in appreciation for his continued service and loyalty. This pistol has never been recovered, and its whereabouts remain unknown to this day. The exact wording of the inscription is also debated among historians and is too vague to quote to you now.

## The Pursuit

The robberies continued for years throughout the south, ultimately culminating in the north, with authorities in full pursuit. The James-Younger Gang robbed banks, railroads, and stagecoaches in Missouri, Kentucky, Tennessee, Iowa, Kansas, Texas, Arkansas, Louisiana, Alabama, and West Virginia.

## The Prison of Minnesota Territory 1876

The dissolution of the James-Younger Gang occurred in 1876, beginning with the capture and subsequent prosecution of both Youngers, and the death of Charlie Pitts. After robbing The First National Bank of Northfield in Minnesota, members split up in an attempt to elude authorities. The Youngers, being at a disadvantage without horses, were easily apprehended. During the robbery that day, a gunfight broke out in the streets of Northfield between gang members and some citizens who'd taken up arms to protect local interests. Caught in the crossfire, an unarmed immigrant from Sweden was killed at the hands of Cole Younger. At the trial, both brothers pleaded guilty to murder to avoid hanging and were sentenced to life terms at the Territorial Prison at Stillwater, Minnesota.

## The Paltry Sum

Having just barely escaped during the Northfield robbery, and still flush with money from past crimes, it was some years before the public would hear from the James-Younger Gang again. In October 1879, the weakened gang resurfaced once more in what they called Little Dixie, where they targeted yet another rail line by robbing the Chicago Alton railroad. Their gang was further diminished, due to the capture of Tucker Basham. This job netted a paltry sum compared to other jobs during the gang's heyday, which led to smaller takes for each of the members. Dissatisfaction began to fester within the ranks, while government pressure to arrest increased, and as a result, the gang's once solid leadership began to crack.

## The Payroll of United States Army Corps of Engineers - 1881

In 1881, Jesse hatched a plan for one final score which would net each member enough money to retire, or at least, that's how he made it seem. He told the other gang members that he knew of an easy mark in North Alabama. He assured the others that they would not regret this final job and quoted to each of them an almost unbelievable bounty to be had. It's not known, to this day, if this was altogether true or just a ruse to secure their assistance. He suggested they'd all go their separate ways after taking an oath of silence. His target was withheld from them until they arrived in Muscle Shoals.

On March 9th, 1881, two days before the robbery, Jesse assembled his extremely shorthanded gang and laid out his plan for robbing the Payroll of the United States Army Corps of Engineers. This daring plan was met with reluctance and raised eyebrows, unlike the enthusiasm routinely exhibited in the past. Even 'The Bull,' Jesse's staunchest supporter, balked at the idea of stealing from such a large government entity and made his reservations known to the others.

This event seems to be the only time Jesse and 'The Bull' did not see eye-to-eye. In fact, Jesse's confidence and his mutual agreement regarding his partner's advice on gang-related matters had never deviated, until now. It was once said that their allegiance was so strong that Jesse sometimes called his partner 'The Bull's Eye' based on the accuracy of his advice. This mutual respect, and their partnership, ended on March 10, 1881.

On that day, the day before the robbery, Jesse attempted to readdress his gang by having them assemble one last time to review their plan. Each man was summoned to the mutually agreed upon location for the meeting, and each man made himself present there, as expected, no less than one hour after the summoning. Every man, except one: The Bull.

## The Phrases-Coined

History has proven that partnerships and gangs come and go, and loyalties wax and wane. Fame also seems to fade over time, but infamy continues to live on, peaking our endless appetites for the unthinkable. More often than not, we find the infamous so intriguing, they leave indelible marks on the very words we speak today.

The Southern-American-English language is rife with slang, especially the dialects spoken by those born and raised in southern states, and those with a southern allegiance, like Jesse James.

One slang word often used, to this day, to express disapproval, disagreement, or regret is simply 'bullshit'.

On that day in 1881, one day before the robbery of the payroll of the United States Army Corps of Engineers was carried out, upon realizing the betrayal and disappearance of his once trusted confidant and gang member The Bull, Jesse James is reported to have remarked, "Bull? Shit!"

No matter where your loyalties lie, I'm sure you've uttered those phrases from long ago, whether it be 'bull's-eye' or 'bull-shit.'

## The Pardon

Jesse would be dead by April of the following year, shot in the head by fellow gang member Bob Ford, never knowing what became of The Bull. Bob Younger was the only gang member to receive a pardon.

## The Posse

As for The Bull, aka Mr. Thorogood Kensington, he returned to his beloved manor house that December. However, his past, including his involvement in the Confederate Ponzi, his affiliation with James-Younger, and his participation in the Philippi Races, regardless of his position on the matter, became the focus of numerous parties in search of justice, bounty, and/or revenge. It was rumored that various amounts of reward money had been offered by multiple jurisdictions for his capture. I, myself, have not yet substantiated these claims, nor have I seen any wanted posters featuring his image.

During those years of the Old West—beginning in 1865, just after the surrender of the Confederate States of America in Virginia, and concluding in the year 1890—the throngs of outlaws that flourished during this time, including the Bushwhackers and the army deserters who roamed the territories unchecked, were relentlessly pursued across America by marshalls and detectives in search of justice.

## **<u>Pinkerton National Detective Agency</u>**

One such agency commissioned for this pursuit was the Pinkerton National Detective Agency. In 1850, Scottish immigrant and entrepreneur, Alan Pinkerton, on seeing a need for tighter security for commercial establishments, especially the railroads, opened one of the first agencies in the United States to support this cause. As this problem grew, due to the lawlessness which burgeoned throughout America, so did the need for a remedy.

ACT 4

# The O'Keefe's and Mr. Standish

**The Passenger Train**

The O'Keefe's arrived at Kensington manor on a Saturday via rail from St. Louis. By happenstance, I walked along the tracks that morning, as I did periodically when other means of clearing my mind had failed. The tracks and locomotives at the station often brought me solace during challenging or unprecedented times.

The decision to accept the position offered to me by Mrs. Kensington was not an easy one. I preferred a life of leisure and solitude. I felt compelled to accept her offer only to perpetuate my lifestyle and because I'd developed a certain fondness for her. I was not ordinarily the type of guy to develop feelings for people, but Mrs. Kensington was different. So I took the job. I hadn't anticipated the stress that accompanies such a position. Maybe I was naive. I envisioned Mrs. Kensington and me living out our days in her manor house alone and undisturbed. But it wasn't panning out that way. She intended on taking in more boarders. More boarders meant more work for me. The burden of responsibility was already taking a toll upon my otherwise easy-going existence. I just wasn't sure I was the guy for the job. Nevertheless, I felt obliged not to let Mrs. Kensington down. I suppose it was the self-doubt that contributed to my melancholy state. And thus, I found myself there on the day they arrived.

That all changed when our gazes met; it was like a reunion of old friends. They had no baggage, making me wonder if it had been lost at some point during their journey. An inquiry into their current state of hunger resulted in an impromptu lunch at the station since I, too, was famished. This is how I spent my time since being designated emissary and envoy to Kensington Manor.

## The Porter

Just as I'd taken my last bite, and only moments after I'd already offered lodging to the O'Keefes on behalf of Mrs. Kensington, I overheard one of the many workers from the Pullman cars speaking in a very derogatory manner about 'the couple from St. Louis who'd just disembarked.' This description, uttered by the porter to a coworker, suited the O'Keefes in nearly all aspects. I suspected his comments concerned them and now regretted my extended invitation for tenancy. Nevertheless, after a brief tour of the Big Easy, I led them back home, where they were introduced to the lady of the house and given their room assignment.

## The Paddleboat

Most times, I was down by the Mississippi on the second Saturday of each spring and summer, where the steam-powered boats moored along the banks of the river, allowing many travelers to experience the Crescent City. Drawn there by the yeasty, sweet smell of the beignets and fresh chicory coffee, I strolled along and hoped for the off-chance I might be able to sample some of the foods. Taking advantage of my current off-duty status, I wandered along the riverbank one morning in anticipation of the first arrivals. After some two hours spent there, suffering from the low country heat, the first of two arrivals pulled alongside for disembarkation. As I often did during the confusion, I boarded unticketed. "Why?" you ask. Well, the boats in the area were widely known for having the finest cuisine in all of New Orleans, and I just couldn't resist. The offering that day consisted of shrimp cocktail, crawfish etouffee, low country boil, jambalaya, and of course, beignets for dessert. I opted for the shrimp and a portion of a beignet. I made my way along the deck toward the gangplank after finishing my meal when suddenly, a man—in fact, a stranger—called out to me:

## The Purser

"Ahoy there, aren't you, Mr. Peabody?"

I did not respond to the strange man as he was unknown to me.

"Cat got your tongue?" He laughed. "Don't mind me, lad. I just noticed you last week when visiting Mrs. Kensington. Tell her I said, 'Hello,' won't you? Thanks, lad. And please sail with us again." He chuckled as I walked away.

I'm a suspicious guy by nature. That's just who I am, and this interaction was just that—suspicious. I don't remember seeing this man at Mrs. Kensington's. Not last week. Not ever. I noticed him behind the glass onboard, making change for the patrons as they approached him single file. How he knew my hostess, I did not know. But naturally, curiosity would build, and I thought about this man daily, trying to place his face while not knowing his identity or modus operandi. I was cautious, being well aware of the old saying, "Curiosity killed the cat."

## The Promenade

I disembarked while trying desperately to recall the stranger at Kensington manor, and before realizing it, I found myself strolling down the Promenade on Canal. Just as I'd turned onto a side street toward the French Quarter, I noticed the same man from the boat as I glanced back over my shoulder. He appeared to be following me.

## The Pursuer

I easily blended into the crowd of this touristy area, losing my pursuer while trying, at the same time, to remain discreet so as not to reveal myself as local. I know this is contrary to the usual advice given to travelers, but I felt it necessary to remain incognito at this juncture of my self-appointed investigation into what had really happened at Kensington Manor.

## The Puppeteer

Up ahead, I noticed a skilled street performer entertaining a group of children with coordinated marionettes. I stopped to take in the show and to take a break from my investigative habits.

## The Prophecy

Before leaving the Quarter, I stopped in for a reading with a local soothsayer, hoping she might shed some light on what had happened. I'd heard of crimes solved in just this manner and felt it worth the time. The medium read the tarot, refusing to make eye contact, and as I watched, this is what she said, "Do not despair. Your destiny will be fulfilled. I see, in your future, a young maiden, many years your junior. She will be wise."

I left immediately afterward with the words of the prophet taken to heart, and while I didn't see this helping the investigation in any way, it was still good to hear. Maybe someday, there'll be a remedy for my loneliness. I'll put my solitary ways behind me.

## The Pirate

Later that evening, after my day out, I dipped into a dimly lit tavern for a nightcap. It was called Jean Leffit's, and I spent numerous evenings here reviewing my many thoughts and clues, trying desperately to pinpoint the exact time and potential cause of the tragedy so that I might exonerate myself and others from this heinous act about which you'll be informed later. As you know, certain details of any investigation are often held close-to-the-vest, and in this case, there is no exception. This is how I spent my time while off-duty from Kensington Manor.

## The Path

My path home that night was an indirect route, so as to confuse anyone who might be tailing me. This was just one of the various methods in my employ to maintain discretion regarding the case.

## The Poydras

My trek took me through the French Quarter, avoiding the Rue Bourbon, detouring up Poydras, veering back to Lasalle, then onto Jackson, destined for the Garden District, and just beyond that, my home at Kensington Manor.

## The Pavillion

I walked the entire way, making a brief stop at the Pavilion Hotel regarding a minor detail pertaining to the investigation. I'd heard through normal channels, commonly known as the grapevine, that a particular individual had recently arrived at the hotel and had not indicated a departure date within the ledger. This detail may or may not be important, but I felt obliged to look into the matter. At first, my interaction with the hotel staff went well enough, but before making any headway, I was invited to leave by the night manager on duty there. This stop provided me with no additional information.

## The Poster

After my departure, as I traversed through the night back toward home, I noticed a poster pasted on the wall, along with many other bulletins and notices, just under the theater's marquee. The colorful artwork, which advertised the matinee currently offered at the cinema, and the reason for my stop there, held my attention only briefly before I noticed a bulletin, which fluttered slightly due to the breeze.

## The Periodical

This bulletin, really more of a clipping from the Times-Picayune, seemed to have been placed by someone investigating the same events about which I sought more detail. No name was attached to the article, but it included a P.O. Box for an address in the Marigny district. I committed the details of the notice to memory, then departed.

## The Paradigm

The next fellow to arrive at our door was different than most. It was difficult for me to determine his origins, but his accent suggested he hailed from the Old Country. To me, his accent was dreadful. At times, I wondered about its authenticity. Was this fellow putting on airs? I suppose it depended upon how you viewed him.

## The Parchment

How did he learn of our residence and the vacancy therein? I still don't know the answer. But his confident nature seemed overpowering, and Mrs. Kensington immediately took a liking to him. He had no baggage but did offer Mrs. Kensington paperwork for review, which I assumed was an application for residency. However, as I listened to her read the document, I got the impression it was a resume that boasted of his lineage from London, England. The more she read, the more it seemed as if this gentleman was descended from royalty, but if that were true, why would he seek boarding at our house? After all, Kensington Manor had seen better days.

## The Park

The next day, I invited this Leopold Standish fellow to lunch in the park, just to get better acquainted. My seniority practically demanded that I be the first to reach out to our new boarder and befriend this newcomer, as any gracious host should. Therefore, a luncheon date was offered but promptly declined, with no reason given. This rejection further raised my suspicions of Mr. Leopold Standish.

## The Pigeons

That afternoon, I left Kensington Manor, destined for the nearest park. The very same park that I'd mentioned to the new boarder earlier that day. Most parks in New Orleans are filled with people and pigeons this time of year, so I had chosen a smaller park visited by fewer individuals, mostly locals.

Upon arriving at the park, and just as I'd expected, I encountered only three individuals present.

*This sparsely populated area should make for a quite enjoyable lunch,* I thought to myself.

The first person I encountered was a lady, obviously a local, dressed in a long, extravagant, pure white gown, with matching gloves and stockings. *A bit overdressed*, I thought, *at least, for midday*. Regardless, she was breathtaking, and most likely, a debutante from one of the many wealthy families in the area.

## The Parasol

Her matching parasol obstructed my view, inhibiting my ability to see the other two individuals. So, as I moved about the park to find just the right area for lunch, I began to inch closer and closer to the couple I had yet to recognize.

## The Pantomime

Suddenly, a juggling performer appeared out of nowhere, dressed in the traditional black and white striped outfit. His performance was interesting and thought-provoking from the very start, just as you might expect, which diverted my attention toward him momentarily. Then, as I continued to search for just the right luncheon spot, I noticed *him*. Now that I had passed by the obstruction of the lady's umbrella, I could see him. It was Mr. Standish, the newest boarder of Kensington Manor and decliner of lunch dates. Puzzled by his presence in the park, I decided to confront his flagrantly rude behavior.

## The Paramour

As I began to make my way toward him, I abruptly realized that he was not alone. The third individual in the park that day seemed to be acquainted with Mr. Standish, and their acquaintance seemed to me to be not that recent. Their mannerisms and their necking and nuzzling of one another suggested to me a paramour relationship. I approached them anyway.

## Penelope

Mr. Standish greeted me as he backed away from the young female, placing a distance of roughly two feet between himself and the girl. The impression I took away from this encounter was that Mr. Standish would prefer this romance remain secretive. I, myself, being the silent type, almost guaranteed it, but he didn't know that. After all, we'd just met mere hours earlier, and as of yet, we did not know one another very well.

Only moments into our conversation, the young individual was introduced to me as, "A friend… Penelope," and he left it at that, offering up no details regarding how they'd met or how long they'd known each other.

## The Pendant

Around her neck, she wore a golden, interlinked choker that contrasted with her coat, and upon the pendant, there seemed to be an engraving. I'd hoped the words upon this adornment would shed more light on their relationship, but I could not see the inscription clearly enough to make any determination.

## The Peridot

The reverse side of the charm that dangled from her chain appeared to be a locket embellished with peridot gemstone the color of her eyes, but no diamonds. This suggested their relationship was one based upon friendship and not one of love, but based on their behavior, I was never too sure.

## The Papillon

Then, just as I bid my newest acquaintance and Mr. Standish farewell, after inviting them both to sup at the manor house, a butterfly flew between us, breaking the monotony. Without a word, Penelope began to chase the beautifully-colored creature through the flowered meadow with Mr. Standish only paces behind. I opted not to pursue them further. There had to be more to their relationship than met the eye.

## The Parfum

As the young couple disappeared around the bend in the stone trail that intersected the park, I was left alone, with only my thoughts and the young lady's scent, which seemed to me a blend of witch hazel and honeysuckle.

## The Perimeter

I exited the park, vainly attempting to get one more glimpse of them before departing. It just didn't make sense to me, and my doubt about them, their origin, and their relationship only intensified. As I passed the gated entrance, I decided to circumvent the perimeter of the park and peered through the railing periodically, in hopes of gaining more insight into their relationship. I'm not at all sure why I was so suspicious; maybe it was just jealousy.

## The Plaza

Ten minutes away by foot, after leaving the friends, or lovers, there in the park, I made my way back toward the manor house, stopping only briefly for lunch at Chartres Street Plaza, since I had not eaten. To my surprise, there they were. It was Leopold and Penelope.

## The Portobello

They were dining there alone, sharing an entree of mushrooms with various side dishes. Now, if I'm not mistaken, this chap seemed somewhat destitute upon his arrival to Kensington manor. How could he afford such an extravagant lunch?

## The Purchase

A meal of this quality must have set the fellow back more than he could afford, based upon his unkempt appearance. So, based on his curious behavior—his preoccupation with his gray suit, the secrecy regarding his love interest, the odd paperwork he presented to Mrs. Kensington at check-in, and his expenditures at the plaza, which obviously exceeded his means—I added Mr. Leopold Standish and Penelope to my list of unvetted suspects.

## The Proboscis

Why so suspicious, you ask? Why so nosey? Well, I've learned you can never be too suspicious when it comes to others. History has proven them to be unreliable, dangerous, deceitful, and heinous. Why so judgmental, you ask? I believe it was a human who once wrote, "Truth is stranger than fiction." If this idiom is true, and I believe it is, then shouldn't I be suspicious, nosey, and judgmental? I defer to your judgment. But please, hold your verdict until you've heard the remaining facts in this investigation.

ACT 5

# MRS. KENSINGTON AND THE WIDOW'S WALK

Night after night, after the others had retired to their quarters, before Mrs. Kensington's threat of eviction, I sat with her, high atop Kensington Manor, on the balcony that overlooked the main grounds of the estate. Here, she bent my ear, talking nearly nonstop, never allowing me to respond to her, although I wanted to do so on many occasions. She made statement after statement and proposed question after question, never varying her statements or questions, ultimately building up to that one interrogative that consumed her thoughts.

"Do you see him? Mr. Peabody?" she asked.

As I gazed out into the distance across Kensington Manor, through the oaks and the Spanish moss, and through the iron gates just at the end of the drive, I could see someone. But it was never him. It was usually just a passerby out for a walk.

"He should be home by now," she often said after asking that first question.

It was heartbreaking to see my lady of the house in such turmoil, but there was nothing I could do for her. I just tried to listen to her and offer her comfort during those trying times. I suppose loneliness and insecurity were the catalyst for Mrs. Kensington's continued intake of boarders.

## Passersby

Not too long after the arrival of Mr. Standish, there came to our door a group of young ladies seeking refuge from the rain that so often fell in our crescent city. Naturally, Mrs. Kensington, due to her kindheartedness, took them in without question. Of course, her offer of refuge was understandable, because I, myself, had seen the rain falling so fast and so furious, it filled the streets within minutes with torrents that moved so rapidly that one could get easily swept away.

I would soon learn the young maidens were Josephine, Ginger, and Molly, three carefree and whimsical girls caught up, by chance, in this ongoing saga.

## The Percent

I'm not one-hundred percent certain, but I believed I might have met Molly prior to this. There was something about her that I couldn't exactly pinpoint, and maybe my inability to do so was hampered by her drenched appearance. Nevertheless, Mrs. Kensington issued room assignments to each of them, like I said, without question.

## Paris

The next night, after the rain from the day before had subsided, as Mrs. Kensington and I sat upon the upper balcony after she'd told me, yet again, about the time she'd spent in Paris with Mr. Kensington on their honeymoon, I learned more details about our three new boarders.

### Pat O'Briens

Josephine, the one with the striking blue eyes that I'd notice almost instantly, even though her soaking wet hair that almost covered her face, was the only out-of-towner. She'd only just met her two companions hours earlier at Mr. O'Brien's Club Tipperary. She'd ducked into the bar to avoid the rain, and coincidentally, was allowed entry due to the continued "storm's brewin'."

Just then, amid her gossip about the new arrivals, Mrs. Kensington blurted out, "Do you see him, Mr. Peabody?"

As usual, I did not see him.

"Does that look like him to you?" she asked.

It did not look like him.

"He should be home soon," she continued.

Then, without warning, she changed the subject again. "You know, that Josephine is older than she looks. She can't hide her age behind those blue eyes."

I did not remark. I'm simply not one for gossip, at least, not in the repeating of it, anyway.

"And, those other two. I'm sure there's a story there," she said.

I continued to listen without interrupting her.

"Is that him, Mr. Peabody?" she exclaimed.

It was not him.

This was, more or less, how our evenings proceeded, prior to Mrs. Kensington's unreasonable demand.

### The Potted Plants

The next evening, during our routine conversation on the balcony, as Mrs. Kensington tended her many plants that sat at the base of the railing, she offered up more details regarding the newest of our housemates.

"Have you had a chance to get acquainted with any of the new girls, Mr. Peabody?"

I did not respond to her. She already knew my feelings about matchmaking.

"I would think an eligible bachelor like yourself would be yearning to fill their dance cards," she continued. "Maybe we should celebrate on behalf of their arrival."

## The Party

The very next evening, attached to the brass knob on the door to my quarters, I found the following invitation:

```
        Greetings from 113 Rue Cheshire
               The Kensingtons
   do hereby request your presence at their home
       for a formal gala to begin at 8:00 pm on
           Sunday, December 10th, 1881
------------------------------------------------------
        ----------------------------
```

## The Primping

After some efforts at grooming to make myself presentable to the attendees of the party to which I had been recently invited, I made my way down the staircase to the grand dining hall. My arrival preceded that of the other guests, and I suppose my earliness was due, in part, to being nervous in my certainty that Mrs. Kensington would attempt to set me up with one of the new girls. She often took it upon herself to match me with eligible young ladies, in the hopes that a budding romance would blossom. And I, being the naturally shy type, never attempted to persuade her otherwise.

I took up a position by the entrance so I might greet the others upon arrival and properly introduce myself like a good under-host should.

When Mrs. Kensington arrived, she addressed me, "Mr. Peabody, you needn't always be so formal. Please go ahead and take your seat."

I obeyed her by retreating from my position at the door and promptly took my seat at the table.

One by one, the other invitees filed into the grand dining hall, ready for their hearty appetites to be satisfied.

After everyone was seated properly, Mrs. Kensington began to serve us, one by one, until all nine of our plates were filled.

## Passion Fruit

"Are you enjoying the appetizer?" Mrs. Kensington asked us. "It's a consommé of passion fruit," she said as she gave a coy glance in my direction. I thought nothing of the comment or the soup, other than noticing she'd never served this particular dish before.

## Pastries

Next, she served us pastries fashioned into the shape of the human heart, embellished with icing in a blood-red color.

"Do you like the desert, Mr. Peabody?" she asked while, once again, smiling at me devilishly, and again, I gave no thought to her comment.

## Parfait

Finally, she placed before each of us a layered pudding concoction. The colors alternated between white and pink, and at the crown, whipped cream with pink berries.

"Well?" she said as she looked around at all of us.

I had no idea what she was trying to ask us.

"Are you ladies and gentlemen enjoying this Valentine's Day Celebration?"

We all just sat there, dumbfounded. It's not because we didn't appreciate the generosity and all the trouble Mrs. Kensington underwent to please us; it was because this was September, not February. But due to our tremendous respect and adoration for her, we said nothing and went along with her misconception.

At the conclusion of another successful, but somewhat odd gala, and after we'd all enjoyed some music from the Victrola, we—that is, Mrs. Kensington and I—retired to the balcony, as usual.

## The Preoccupation

As I sat there beside Mrs. Kensington that evening, as she droned on and on about the same old subjects, I couldn't help my preoccupation with 'Molly,' feeling like I must have met her at some point in the past. I was certain I'd seen the face, the eyes, and the hair before, and not just on that rainy night when she'd come to our door with her friends, but on some other occasion I couldn't recall. I did notice an oddity that had occurred earlier that evening during the gala, where Mr. Standish had interacted with everyone present, excluding this one called 'Molly,' and as I watched the two of them, they seemed to speak to one another, but only with their eyes. I didn't draw any conclusions until later that night in my room.

## Pacific SS - Collins Line

"Are you listening, Mr. Peabody?" Mrs. Kensington asked.

I was embarrassed to answer her, so I redirected my attention and nodded my head.

"Anyway, as I was saying… Mr. Kensington and I visited

many places abroad, after taking the SS Pacific to Europe. It was a magical time."

*Here we go again*, I thought to myself as Mrs. Kensington continued to embellish her tale with the details of her travels with Mr. Kensington.

"Did you enjoy the festivities tonight, Mr. Peabody? You know, you have to put forth an effort. I think Ginger is the one for you."

I neither confirmed nor denied an interest in Ginger, nor did I confirm or deny any interest in any of the others. I simply listened without interrupting, as I thought about that idiosyncratic, and dare I say pedestrian, human tendency to name others after their hair color.

## **The Pinpoint**

Later that night, after returning to my room slightly later than usual, with the events of the gala still swimming in my head, I attempted to organize the details of that night in chronological order, a retracing of footsteps, so to speak. This method of recollection has been an old tried and true method of recalling certain important elements of an event or occurrence that may linger in one's mind due to fuzziness. After debating silently to myself within my head, I finally realized where I'd seen this 'Molly' before. I'd been introduced to her recently, but she'd been introduced to me as 'Penelope.'

I'm sure you can imagine how this elevated my curiosity to a dangerous—and possibly, even deadly—level. I just had to know why the two of them—Leopold and 'Molly,' or 'Penelope,' whichever it was—would perpetuate such a ruse.

## **The Pragmatic**

Maybe I should've handled this event differently. Maybe not. I'm still unsure.

I debated the issue with myself, as I usually did whenever I was unsure about what I should do. Should I risk offending the new housemates by prying into their private lives? Or, should I just ignore my curiosity? I wasn't sure either way. Nevertheless, I had to get to the root cause of this deception, no matter the cost.

My theory was as follows: Mrs. Kensington, being a very practical and religious woman, forbade the intermingling of non-married individuals at Kensington Manor. The O'Keefes, the only pair to cohabitate within the same room, were, by all outward appearances, a couple, and they shared surnames. This could imply a brother and sister relationship, a father and daughter relationship, or they might just be related to one another as cousins. My determination, based upon Mrs. Kensington's comments, was to regard the two as husband and wife.

I'd often heard her say, "Don't the O'Keefes make a lovely couple?" Followed by, "Aren't those two, dreamy? Mr. Kensington and I used to be like that."

Therefore, I'd determined that the O'Keefes were, indeed, a couple legally bound by matrimony.

How does this apply to Mr. Standish, you may ask?

Well, I'd determined him to be somewhat of a 'playboy' a 'tomcat,' if you will. His excessive complimentary comments toward all of the girls, coupled with his constant worry over his appearance, could mean only one thing. This chap wanted to play the field. More than likely, he had multiple love interests. The arrival of 'Molly,' or 'Penelope,' at the manor house was coincidental, and quite likely, putting a crimp in his plan. I further determined his standoffish behavior toward her at the gala was a dead giveaway regarding his plan. Caught unprepared, he didn't know how to react to her presence in the house, and he wouldn't allow Mrs. Kensington to become aware of their relationship. If she learned of the affair, one of them, either Leopold or Molly—or Penelope, or whoever she was—would find themselves seeking another refuge.

At this point, even though I had no evidence against him, I was reluctant to exonerate Mr. Leopold Standish.

## The Protestant

You may remember I've mentioned Mrs. Kensington was a religious woman. Every Sunday, come rain or shine, she engaged in her religion by reading from her Bible.

## Proverbs

I awoke sometime in the night for no particular reason, other than to relieve myself, and as I walked down the hall past Mrs. Kensington's room on my left, I noticed a light underneath her door.

Not because I wanted to invade her privacy, but because I was concerned for her well-being, I approached her door for a quick listen. This is what I heard:

"And why wilt thou, my son, be ravished with a strange woman, and embrace the bosom of a stranger? Proverbs 5:20."

"Did you hear that?" she asked.

This sudden question terrified me; she knew I was just outside her door listening. How could I overcome such an awkward and embarrassing event?

Just as I was about to knock, I heard her voice again.

"Did you, Mr. Kensington?"

Upon hearing the repeated question, I refrained from knocking and just stood there silently.

Based on the monologue I heard from behind her door that night, and on many subsequent Sunday nights that followed, this is my conclusion:

Mrs. Kensington, I suppose due to her loneliness, conversed with her dead husband by reading the Bible to him at night in the solitude of her room. She would read a verse, ask him a question, sometimes more than once, and then debate the unheard answer. Don't be mistaken when I say, 'unheard.' What I mean to imply is that the response was 'unheard' by me. To Mrs. Kensington, the response was loud and clear.

## The Prostitutes

On several occasions, I also witnessed her soliciting much-needed advice from the former man of the house.

"Do you think any of the new girls are prostitutes, Mr. Kensington?"

I was shocked upon hearing this question because if it were, indeed, true, I'd missed it completely. And if I'd missed it completely, then I must not be much of an investigator.

My conclusion from this Sunday night episode was as follows:

Mrs. Kensington knew that Mr. Kensington was, in fact, dead and never returning to Kensington Manor—at least, not returning in the flesh. However, she sought his advice and approval on taking us into her home. Most of the Biblical verses seemed to promote her willingness to keep us there, but only if she had his approval.

These newly acquired details began to shift the focus of my investigation.

First of all, why did Mrs. Kensington continue to assume that every individual who passed by our gate was, in fact, her dead husband? Was she also perpetuating some ruse for deception, or was she the victim of a declining mental state? Second, during her Sunday night conversations with Mr. Kensington, I never heard him express any dissatisfaction with us residing in his home. I know what you're thinking, and of course, I didn't hear Mr. Kensington say anything, but I did hear the other side of these 'conversations,' and from this, I was able to deduce that dead Mr. Kensington had no issues with Mrs. Kensington's living arrangements.

## Pontchartrain Lake

Seven days later, after listening to the Victrola which followed the routine gala, Mrs. Kensington was at it again.

"Is that him, Mr. Peabody?"

By this time, can you imagine what I was thinking? My gut instinct told me she was faking this entire thing. I mean, really. Repeating 'Is that him?' over and over seemed somewhat psychotic to me. On the other hand, elderly folks have been known to talk out-of-their-heads during their old age. Maybe, just maybe, this was the case for Mrs. Kensington. But if that were true, why did her awareness change from gala to balcony to Bible reading?

"Have I ever told you about Mr. Kensington's love for the water, Mr. Peabody?"

Surprisingly, she had not.

"Mr. Kensington wanted to be a sailor; you know. Before he was called up in the war."

I'd never heard this one before.

"He often sailed the waters on Lake Pontchartrain… He loved that old boat."

## Padre Island

"He took it out on the ocean one time. Did I ever tell you about that, Mr. Peabody?"

She had not.

"He was inexperienced back then. That's why he hired Cajun Jack."

This was news to me.

"His father bought the boat over in Texas and hired Jack to sail her back home. Did I ever tell you about her, Mr. Peabody? Mr. Kensington christened her *Onomatopoeia*. He loved that boat.

"Oh, how I missed him while he was gone. That's when I took up the wheel. They say it's good to have a hobby, you know, to keep your mind off things."

*The wheel?* I thought to myself. I'd never known Mrs. Kensington to drive.

### The Preserves and the Pottery Wheel

"That wheel helped me through many lonely times. Of course, I did other things, you know. I put up some preserves, mostly blackberry, and I 'piddled' in the garden, but it was my pottery wheel that kept me going. I made the vase on the mantle myself; you know."

### Peonies and Peace Lilies

"And my flowers, oh, they were so beautiful. Let's see now… I grew peonies, lilies, roses, tulips, jimson, and many other varieties. Of course, I had help, you know. Mr. Brooks helped me in the garden when he wasn't busy forging something for Mr. Kensington."

Then after an indeterminate time of silent reflection, she continued, "I suppose those days are gone forever, Mr. Peabody."

### The Pros and Cons

By this time the status of my investigation was scattered all over the board. Speaking of 'boards,' I even considered consulting Mrs. Kensington's old Ouija board for advice, but then I had second thoughts.

As the evening concluded and I returned to my room, I began to put together a summary of just where I stood in this ongoing investigation. The Pros and Cons were as follows:

In the Cons column, I'd yet to determine if a crime had been committed at all. I did suspect that Mr. Kensington had not died of natural causes. Without a crime, how could I have suspects? That, too, was a con.

Most great inspectors have strong feelings when conducting their investigations—hunches, they call them. I also had strong feelings about this case. I suspected that Mr. Kensington had been murdered, and the motive for his killing had been robbery. More specifically, I believed someone had targeted him for the alleged gold in the safe behind the portrait that hung over the mantle. Therefore, my suspect list continued to grow, as no one had been alibied or exonerated.

As for the Pros, well… The only one I could think of was having me, Jasper Peabody, on the case as a self-appointed, professional, private investigator.

ACT 6

# Revenge of the Sultana

After his self-prescribed demotion from Private to Mister, after being discovered unconscious in the pumpkin patch near the Fontineax Plantation, and after leaving the care of his nursemaid, Yvonne, Mr. Kensington did not make it very far before he was surrounded by troops from both the North and the South. As he continued west on his mount, the wayward horse he'd inherited as a result of some rider's unfortunate death, he began to feel an all-consuming paranoia of his imminent arrest by the Confederacy for deserting his post, or arrest by the Union for being a Confederate.

**<u>The Parish, St. Landry</u>**

As he approached the St. Landry Parish of Louisiana that November, he heard the thunderous booms from the cannons and the roars from the charging troops in the distance, and Mr. Kensington made an impromptu and strategic decision that altered his course in life.

Terrified as he continued onward, Mr. Kensington dismounted and then slapped his steed upon the rear, sending her galloping away. There, just at the battlefield's edge, and dead, as dead can be, lay several Union soldiers.

After a few seconds spent sizing up each man, Mr. Kensington began to remove the uniform of the man whose size most closely matched his own. Next, he removed his own gray clothing, ultimately swapping his uniform for the uniform of the dead Union soldier. Then, he began to employ the next step of his cleverly designed ruse.

Due to his innate ability to determine troop movements, even before the occurrence, he knew the Union territory on which he stood would soon be occupied by the Confederates. He also knew how he'd be treated were his true identity and his true status of 'deserter' to become known. He did not want to end up in chains at Andersonville, where he'd be hated by both the North and the South.

Therefore, he decided to pose as a Union soldier, in hopes that his capture would result in his transfer to the nearby Cahaba prison in Dallas County, Alabama, where he'd continue to hold out until the end of the war, which he estimated would arrive sooner rather than later.

## The Prediction

The Battle of Carrion Crow Bayou on November 3rd, 1863 was, indeed, a Confederate victory, just as Mr. Kensington had predetermined. Also, and just as he'd predicted, Mr. Kensington was captured and subsequently transferred to Alabama.

## The Prison

Prison life in Dallas County at Cahaba was not as pleasant as the manor life Mr. Kensington had once known, but it was much better than the deplorable conditions and treatment experienced by men incarcerated at Andersonville.

The Prison at Cahaba, not very far from Selma, was relatively new and home to approximately 300 or so men on the date of his arrival. Luckily, Mr. Kensington encountered no other Confederates known to him, making his ruse a rather easy venture. His identity was recorded as follows: Sergeant Boyette Caldwell of the Union infantry. His self-proclaimed promotion from Mister to Sergeant was well-warranted since he'd been overlooked for promotion numerous times by the South.

By August 1864, the population at Cahaba had doubled, and with each new intake of prisoners, Mr. Kensington worried about being recognized. He'd traveled to many northern cities in his youth, following in his father's footsteps as a young man and learning the family business. This led him to Philadelphia, Chicago, New York, and as far north as Boston, where he'd met many Yankee men now serving their country as Union soldiers. It was only a matter of time before he became known to his captors.

## The Pivot

In just one month, April 1865, the tides of history pivoted away from the evil and inhumane abuses inflicted by one man onto another, in favor of a more righteous civilization. This sequence of defining moments in the history of the United States occurred within just thirty days.

## Pickett, General George

The Battle of Five Forks occurred on April 1, 1865, concluding with a Union victory when Confederate General George Pickett, on direct orders from Robert E. Lee, failed to defend the area. This resulted in the capture of nearly 4,000 Confederates and the fall of Petersburg and Richmond, Virginia, thus initiating the Confederacy's final retreat.

## Petersburg, Virginia

After the fall of Richmond and Petersburg, Union troops engaged the retreating Confederates almost immediately on April 6 at the 1865 Battle of Sailor's Creek.

## Paine's Cross Roads

As Confederate troops, extremely weakened from consecutive defeats and undernourished from lack of supplies, continued to retreat, they were buoyed by hopes of being resupplied near Amelia Springs. Sadly, their expectation of a rendezvous with wagon trains carrying ammunition and food was foiled when Union soldiers, led by Brigadier General Henry E. Davies attacked and destroyed this Confederate supply line at Paine's Cross Road.

## Parker, Ely S.

On April 9, 1865, General Robert E. Lee surrendered in Virginia at Appomattox Courthouse. The surrender, along with its terms and conditions, was recorded by Ely S. Parker, adjutant to General Ulysses S. Grant. Afterward, at approximately four p.m., a wave of revelry rising within the Union ranks was squashed upon General Grant's order. He was reported to have said:

**"The Confederates are now our countrymen, and we do not want to exult over their downfall."**

## The Play

Five days later, on April 14, 1865, President Lincoln would be assassinated. Not all countrymen viewed the preservation of the

Union as graciously as General Grant, giving birth to unorganized, sporadic attacks of revenge and retribution.

## The Paddle Boat

April 27, 1865 marks the largest maritime disaster in the history of the United States, even outpacing that of the Titanic. Here's what happened:

Now that the war was over, just as Mr. Kensington had predicted, the release and repatriation of all prisoners, both Confederate and Union, became a mammoth undertaking.

The USS Sultana, a wooden, side-wheeled, steam-driven paddle boat was commissioned in 1863 and began operating on a routine route from St. Louis, Missouri to New Orleans, Louisiana, transporting cotton, coal, sugar, and passengers between the two cities. But that was not its cargo on that fateful day.

## Passage

Just weeks after the conclusion of the American Civil War, there arose a tremendous need for passage and transportation up and down the Mississippi River for those men, both Union and Confederate, who needed repatriation.

The USS Sultana left St. Louis on April 13th, 1865, destined for New Orleans, where she was to be employed to fulfill this need. Simultaneously, news of Lee's surrender and the assassination of Abraham Lincoln was just reaching the staff and inmates at Cahaba prison in Dallas County, Alabama where preparations were initiated to process and discharge both active-duty soldiers and prisoners for their return home. Mr. Kensington, still successful in maintaining his ruse and his anonymity, was one of those men.

## The Parole

Based on Mr. Kensington's identification as a Union soldier and based on the terms of surrender agreed upon at Appomattox, all the inmates incarcerated in Cahaba, Alabama, including Mr. Kensington, were granted unconditional parole and transport to Vicksburg, Mississippi, where they would be ferried either North or South via the Mississippi River.

## The Pressure

On April 21, 1865, the Sultana arrived in New Orleans and unloaded the various cargoes. There, she was reprovisioned for her return to St. Louis, departing with an extremely limited return cargo in anticipation of filling the ship's hold at Vicksburg with recently released soldiers destined for disbursement at varying points north along the Mississippi.

## Propulsion

Just prior to arriving in Vicksburg, the Sultana developed propulsion issues due to a leak that formed in one of the ship's four boilers. The boat's diminished mobility resulted in a late arrival in Vicksburg, and a mechanic was dispatched to evaluate and repair the leak.

## Packed

As the repair was underway, the Sultana was loaded with over 2,200 Union soldiers and former prisoners, grossly exceeding the boat's suggested capacity of 376. In addition to these parolees, the vessel also held 300 more individuals, made up of civilian passengers and crew. The Sultana departed Vicksburg on April 24, 1865, packed well beyond its limits.

## The Precipitation

For two days, the Sultana struggled upriver, traveling against an unusually strong current that had developed when spring rainfall had swollen the river to near-record highs. The constant stoking of the boilers depleted the ship's coal reserve rapidly, and plans were made to take on more coal from barges upriver, just beyond Memphis, Tennessee.

After a brief stop to offload approximately 200 men who lived in that general vicinity, the Sultana continued to make her way north. Just seven miles upstream, north of Memphis, at approximately two a.m., the Sultana was rocked by a series of explosions. These immediately destroyed a large portion of the ship, including the upper decks and bridge, reducing the formerly beautiful ship to a wayward, burning heap, still afloat, but drifting out of control on the river.

## The Percussion

The explosion was heard for miles and was so powerful, many of the passengers riding on the exposed decks were catapulted into the river.

## The Plumes

The wooden construction of the Sultana acted as fodder for the flames, as plumes of smoke and ash billowed high above the burning remains.

## The Pocahontas

The Pocahontas, as well as numerous other vessels sailing the Mississippi at that time, were quickly dispatched in a hasty attempt to rescue the individuals who had survived the explosions. Seven hours later, after the flaming wreck of the Sultana had drifted approximately six miles, she sank near the west bank of the Mississippi at Mound City, Arkansas.

## The Prisoners

Most of the prisoners onboard that day were either killed instantly or died from smoke inhalation, captive on the boat as it drifted aimlessly.

## The Panic

The panic from the explosions and fire caused many individuals to 'abandon ship,' after which they perished in the cold water of the Mississippi.

## The Perished

Estimates of those who perished range from approximately 1,500 to over 1,800.

## The Private

As I mentioned earlier, just hours before consecutive explosions ultimately sank the Sultana, approximately 200 men disembarked at Memphis. All 200 men wore navy blue coats, designating them as Union soldiers, but only 199 of them actually were; the 200th man was Private Thorogood Kensington.

## <u>The Patriotic</u>

If history has proven anything, it's that patriots come in all colors. To some, allegiance to country, and a willingness to die and kill to maintain that allegiance, can drive men to do extraordinary things; it can also drive men to do heinous things.

If Private Kensington had been captured by Union troops prior to the deception he'd employed to hide his identity, he would have been released into the public conditionally, and only after recitation of the required oath pledging his allegiance to the Union of the United States of America. Since there was no capture of him by the Union, and since his capture was at the hands of Confederates, there was no condition of release and no pledge to the Union. Perhaps, his ensuing actions were, therefore, patriotic—at least, to him.

As the Union prisoners made their way from Alabama to Vicksburg for transport up the Mississippi, Mr. Kensington became acquainted with a fellow prisoner who'd recently been captured and incarcerated. This man attempted to engage Sergeant Caldwell, aka Thorogood Kensington, on several occasions, only to be rebuffed repeatedly, before forcing his hand. Mr. Kensington was made aware, in a direct and matter-of-fact way, that the concealment of his true identity was not as secure as he'd thought, and that the disclosure of his true identity and its continued concealment might be in jeopardy.

## <u>The Perjury</u>

Upon entrance to Cahaba prison months prior, Mr. Kensington had made certain concessions by agreeing to no longer take up arms against the South, which he already had no intentions of doing, but he'd also lied to his captors about his identity and his allegiance, which could compromise his future. His capture while dressed in Blue, and his proffer of false identification, could be misconstrued. Questions might be asked. *Where did this sergeant's allegiance lie? Was it with the North from the very start? Was he a Union Spy?*

Would these accusations ever come to light? Mr. Kensington hoped not. Did his acquaintance die onboard the Sultana? He wasn't one-hundred percent sure.

Mr. Kensington's recent acquaintance had demanded money, with the intention of blackmail, and even though Mr. Kensington was no spy at all, his deception would have been difficult to explain.

Days later, after the sinking, and after stealing some civilian clothing and shedding the Union uniform, Mr. Kensington headed west under the assumption that he was now in the clear.

## The Penny Press

Across the river now, and well into Missouri, Mr. Kensington took up shelter in a small boarding house under his true identity, without divulging any additional details about himself or his past.

The next morning, on the floor of his room, he found a news bulletin that had been prepared and printed by a local penny press and slipped beneath his door sometime during the night.

Now days old, but still on the front page, it contained news and theories regarding the sinking of the Sultana.

He departed that night, heading northwest, making it all the way to Liberty, Missouri before seeking refuge in another small boarding house in town.

Here, he remained alone, holed up within his room, not even seeing the light of day for weeks at a time.

On the 13th of February, 1866, Mr. Kensington was awakened by an ongoing disturbance in the streets of Liberty, just outside his window. Galloping horses, yelling, and a flurry of gunfire could be heard throughout the small town. When it was all over, Mr. Kensington would learn from the townsfolk that their bank, the Clay County Savings Association had been robbed, leaving one teenage boy dead in the street.

Later that summer, in nearby Jackson County, Missouri, another bank robbery, theorized to be perpetrated by the same men, left another man dead and another bank empty. Recognizing one man's name, to whom the robberies had been attributed, Mr. Kensington remained in the Missouri area, on and off, for the next eight years, hoping to join up with these outlaws. The name he'd recognized was Quantrill. He'd heard of this man leading a band of marauders on their campaign of robbery and revenge against the North. Since Mr. Kensington was now a criminal himself, and in need of money, he waited for his opportunity.

ACT 7

# (THE RAINBOW)

During the sixteen years of 1865 to 1881, beginning with the end of the American Civil War and ending with Mr. Kensington's return to his Manor home in Louisiana, Mrs. Kensington knew nothing regarding his whereabouts. Even to this day, those whereabouts have been widely debated. It was during this same time period that Mrs. Kensington resided alone in the manor house, awaiting her husband's safe return from the war, and wondering about those aforementioned whereabouts. It was also during this time that many curious inquirers found their way to the gates of Kensington manor, seeking information on these whereabouts.

## **The Gray**

In 1864, Mrs. Kensington was summoned to her front door by a tremendous pounding upon the entranceway. There, she found a Confederate major, accompanied by a small party of soldiers of lesser rank, which included one captain, two sergeants, and eight privates. The major, still perched in the saddle on his mount, began questioning her regarding Mr. Kensington.

Mrs. Kensington brusquely interrupted him, saying, "Thorogood isn't hurt, is he?"

"Ma'am, I'm Major Barfield, and this is Captain Maxwell. How did you know we were here for Thorogood?"

"Who else would you be inquiring about at my door? Thorogood is the only Confederate soldier I know."

"And what is your relation to Mr. Thorogood Kensington?"

"He's my husband," Mrs. Kensington replied. "Is he well?"

"That's what we're trying to determine, Ma'am. When was the last time you saw him or corresponded with him?"

"I haven't seen Thorogood since the day he left for war…" She hesitated. "That was in 1861."

"How about wires or letters? Have you received any correspondence from him?"

"No, I haven't." She scowled. "Hasn't he been with you?"

"No Ma'am… I'm sorry to have to tell you this, Ma'am, but his commanding officer has reported him missing."

"Missing?"

"Yes, Ma'am," the major replied. He added, "Ma'am, how is it that a private in the Army of the Confederacy has such an elaborate home? Most soldiers, particularly the ones holding the rank of private, come from modest and humble origins."

Mrs. Kensington was too shocked to respond initially.

"Ma'am, did you hear me? Can you explain how you all came about this big, fancy home?"

"This home was a gift to Thorogood and me, a wedding gift, given to us by his father."

"Is his father still living?"

"No, he passed away suddenly, just after my marriage to his son. Some people say, 'That marriage killed him.' Is Thorogood dead, Major?"

"Now, I didn't say that, Ma'am. At this point, he's just missing."

"And you think he's here?"

The major just smiled as he remained on horseback, before asking, "Do you mind if we look around, Ma'am?"

"I told you, he's not here."

"Then you won't mind… Correct, Ma'am"

The major immediately gave the sign to his men to begin searching, while providing Mrs. Kensington with no further details regarding their investigation and giving her no opportunity to respond.

This Confederate search party, headed up by Major Barfield, returned numerous times to Kensington Manor to search for the private, never once finding any evidence pertaining to his whereabouts.

## **The Blue**

Three years later, in 1867, a search party in Blue arrived at Kensington manor with outlandish accusations, misidentifications, and charges. Arriving at Mrs. Kensington's door that day was an enormous party in search of one man who might have information vital to the Union effort. This party of nearly forty was led by a general, one major, and two captains. The rest of the party was made up of sergeants, corporals, and privates. They towed two wagons behind them, one of which held an enclosure made from iron bars.

Just as before, once Mrs. Kensington had opened her door, the questioning began.

"Hello, I'm General Ambrose Burnside. My men and I are here in search of an individual, and we thought you might be able to help."

"What makes you think I might help?" Mrs. Kensington replied.

"Well, this man was last seen at Cahaba Prison over in Alabama. That's not all that far from here," General Burnside said, suspicion lacing his tone. "This man was dressed in a Blue Union uniform bearing a sergeant's insignia. When asked, this man said his name was Boyette Caldwell, but we think this man's name was really Thorogood Kensington. Isn't that your husband?"

"That's my husband's name, but my husband was a Confederate Private. You've been misled, General."

"I don't think I have," General Burnside replied. "This information has been provided to us by reliable sources. As I said, this man was seen over in Alabama, then again, in Vicksburg, Mississippi. Is your husband at home?"

"I haven't seen Thorogood since 1861. He was killed," Mrs. Kensington replied.

"Do you have some correspondence reporting your husband as killed-in-action?"

"No Sir, I do not. I was told about Thorogood by a Confederate major."

"What was this major's name?"

"I don't recall. It was some time ago."

The accompanying major in the party spoke up, "Ma'am, this information is vital to your freedom."

"Major," General Burnside barked as he interrupted the Major, "I don't think we need to threaten the lady, do we?" The General raised his eyebrows as he tilted his head in Mrs. Kensington's direction.

General Burnside and his men found no evidence of any Boyette Caldwell or Thorogood Kensington that day.

This party would return to Kensington Manor in subsequent years, at variable intervals, in search of Thorogood Kensington, aka Boyette Caldwell.

## The Red

In 1875, Mrs. Kensington was visited again, this time, by a less organized group of men known by some as 'Jayhawkers,' and known by others as 'Red Legs.' These vigilante men, rivals of the 'Bushwhackers' had taken it upon themselves to search for and to flush out any remaining Confederate sympathizers or individuals whose post-war abilities, resources, or actions might weaken the Union. In doing so, while they had good intentions, they sank to the same level as those they sought to snuff out. In fact, on that day in 1875, the 'Red Legs,' disappointed by their inability to find any Confederates holed up at Kensington Manor, burned the few out-buildings and structures that had survived the war. The smokehouse, the barn, the stable, and the icehouse were destroyed.

## The Pink

In 1880, just one year prior to Mr. Kensington's return to Kensington Manor, Mrs. Kensington was visited by a small, but eloquent group of young men, all donning the highest quality of clean, pressed suits. These men, who arrived there on horseback, knocked on the front door of Kensington Manor, looking for a man known as 'the Bull.'

"Good morning, Ma'am. My name is Alan Pinkerton, and these are my sons, Robert and William." He indicated two of the men standing with him before pointing toward the third. "The gentleman to Robert's left is Edward Rucker. We're agents of the Pinkerton Detective Agency. Maybe you've heard about us?"

"No, I don't believe I have," Mrs. Kensington replied. "Detectives, you say?"

"Yes, Ma'am. We've worked for many prestigious clients, including the Union Army and Abraham Lincoln."

"I suppose you're looking for Thorogood, too?" Mrs. Kensington replied, seemingly unimpressed.

"Is Thorogood your husband?"

"Yes, he is," Mrs. Kensington responded.

"When did you last see Thorogood?"

"It's been almost twenty years; 1861, I think."

"Does your husband have any sort of nickname, or maybe, an alias that he uses?"

"If you're referring to the name of Boyette Caldwell, then I suppose, he does. That's what I've been told, anyway."

"Told, Ma'am?" Allan Pinkerton prompted.

"Yes, and by government agents. Surely, you men know about that, if you've worked for the Union Army as you claim."

"When did you last speak to representatives from the Union Army?" Mr. Rucker asked.

"Off and on over the years. I don't exactly keep track," Mrs. Kensington said.

"Well, as we stated, we are agents of the Pinkerton Detective Agency, currently contracted on assignment with the United States Justice Department. May we come in?"

"Mr. Kensington doesn't like visitors in his home."

"I thought you said you haven't seen him."

"I haven't…" she prevaricated. "He still doesn't allow visitors in his home. Those were his rules and I still abide by them."

"Other than this 'Boyette Caldwell,' does he have any other aliases?"

"Well, before the war, the men in his hunting group called him something. Let me see… What was it?" Mrs. Kensington said as she thought out loud.

"It's very important, Ma'am," Robert Pinkerton added.

"Oh, yes, that's it. They called him 'Rhino'."

"Rhino?" Allan repeated.

"Yes," Mrs. Kensington confirmed.

"How did your husband acquire such a moniker?"

"From the kill."

"Kill? I'm afraid I don't follow you, Ma'am."

At this point, Mrs. Kensington invited all of the men from the

Pinkerton Agency into her home and led them to the mount on the wall in Mr. Kensington's former study. As they stood there before the enormous rhinoceros' head, she explained, "Thorogood was the only one to get a kill on safari. I forget what year it was, but he was gone for nearly three months. And this is why. I hate that ugly thing, but he was so proud of it. And, now… I just can't bear the thought of removing it from the house."

"Is there anything else you can tell us about this, Ma'am?"

"I don't believe so. As I said, he killed this white bull rhinoceros on safari, and ever since, that's what they called him."

"Bull, or Rhino? The man we're looking for has been known to go by 'Bull.'"

"No one called him that, to my knowledge, but it was a male rhino."

The Pinkerton men left Kensington Manor, believing they were on the right track.

## **The Green**

In December of 1881, years after Mrs. Kensington had given up hope of ever seeing her husband again, after the manor house had fallen further into decline, and after Mrs. Kensington had determined her husband was no patriot, an unexpected visitor arrived at the door of her manor house.

Mrs. Kensington opened the door that day to a slender and bearded man, approximately her age; a man she, at first, did not recognize.

"Are you looking for Thorogood, too?" she asked the stranger.

"Don't you recognize me, Annie?" Thorogood Kensington asked.

She stood there, studying the man who'd just called her Annie. Only one person she'd ever known had called her by that name.

"I can't believe the house is still here, that they didn't burn it down," Mr. Kensington said as he looked the house up and down while running his hands over the paint-chipped columns that once gleamed brightly with perfection.

"Thorogood? Is that you?" Mrs. Kensington finally asked him.

The man turned toward her, removed his hat, and pulled back his long hair and beard, attempting to reveal as much of his face as possible.

That's when the tears began to flow.

That night, after Mr. Kensington had bathed for the first time in weeks, the Kensingtons, in an attempt to relive the past, and in an attempt to return to the joy that'd once known together, planned and participated in what would be their final gala together, just the two of them. And just as you might expect, upon the knob to Mr. Kensington's study, Mrs. Kensington placed an elaborate invitation that read:

```
          Greetings from 113 Rue Cheshire
                  The Kensingtons
     do hereby request your presence at their home
       for a formal gala to begin at 8:00 pm on
             Sunday, December 10th, 1881
------------------------------------------------------------

          ------------------------------
```

Over the next two hours, the two of them reveled in each other's company, behaving almost like newlyweds as they ate the modest meal and then waltzed, just like they'd done so many years ago. Then, just as the Victrola slowed to a distorted halt, Mr. Kensington abruptly changed.

"Where are they?" he demanded, as he shifted from waltzer to madman and grabbed her by both of her arms.

"Who?" Mrs. Kensington asked with fear now upon her face.

"The letters." Mr. Kensington demanded, "Have you shown the letters to anyone?"

"What letters?"

"The letters I sent to you over the years. Where are they?"

Mr. Kensington's impatience continued to terrify his wife. He was unaware of his wife's diminished mental capacity, something that sometimes occurs as we age and affects our ability to remember things, and assumed she was being deceitful.

"I don't know anything about any letters. I haven't seen or heard from you since you left here for the war… Where have you been? Is it over?" Mrs. Kensington asked.

"Is what over?" Mr. Kensington replied.

"The war?"

It finally hit him. His wife wasn't her former self. She couldn't tell him where the letters were because she couldn't remember even receiving them. He was still unaware of the many visitors who had come to their door seeking his whereabouts during his absence.

The human mind is funny that way. One minute, it can recall something that happened many years ago. The next minute, it can't remember yesterday. This cycle of what we can remember and what we can't remember is sometimes patternistic, but other times, it has no rhythm or beat that can be counted. There one moment, and gone the next.

Mr. Kensington spent much of his time during the many months that followed doing only two things: caring for Mrs. Kensington and searching Kensington Manor for those letters.

On late afternoons, when they engaged in high tea, Mrs. Kensington often remarked on their estate, pointing out obvious things that she noticed.

"The grass is not as green as it used to be, wouldn't you agree, Thorogood?"

"Yes, Annie, I do agree."


## The Yellow


The days came and went, just like Mrs. Kensington's memory, with her being able to recall the intricate details regarding their honeymoon in Paris, but not being able to remember the where-abouts of the letters. And on several occasions, even though Mr. Kensington knew of and acknowledged his wife's dementia, he still pleaded with her to tell him where she'd hidden the letters.

One summer's night, in 1882, as the couple sat on the balcony, Mr. Kensington confessed to his wife, "Annie, I've done some awful things. Some of those things, I told you about in the letters. Some of those things, I've never told you. It would not be good for me if those letters fell into the wrong hands. Can't you just try to remember?

In response, she continued to comment on the appearance of the estate. It was as if his pleas had fallen upon deaf ears. That's just the way it is sometimes when conversing with someone in this condition. Mr. Kensington's words that night were nothing more than a soliloquy.

## The Blue again

The next day proved to be a beautiful southern summer's day. The sky was blue over Kensington manor, but this was not uplifting to the man of the house. He was blue because he had not yet found those letters.

## The Rainbow

Despite this beautiful day, Kensington Manor suffered from an absence of color. The flowered grounds that formerly burst with vibrant colors spanning the spectrum of the rainbow were now bleak and without hue.

## The Black

Because of the dreary and rundown appearance of his formerly exquisite home, because of his inability to find those letters, and due to his inability to open his safe, Mr. Kensington fell into a black mood, where he remained for many months.

ACT 8

# THE 'CRASH' OF THE ONOMATOPOEIA

Just weeks after entering into the bonds of holy matrimony and just days after moving into Kensington Manor, Mr. Kensington departed Louisiana, bound for the coast of Texas where his father had found and purchased a mid-sized schooner, including all of the sails and rigging.

## The Petty Officer

Thorogood was informed of this event via telegraph and ordered by his father to proceed in haste to South Padre Island, Texas for a 'crash' course in navigation, rigging, and other general principles in sailing. The elder Kensington also demanded that he bring along Cajun Jack, the blacksmith at Kensington Manor and former Petty Officer in the French Navy.

Thorogood was further instructed to sail the boat back to Pontchartrain Lake, with Jack acting as skipper.

So, in compliance with his father's orders, Thorogood made arrangements to travel to Texas and take ownership of his new boat, bringing Jack along and leaving livery and stable hand, Pearson Brooks at the manor house to perform any smithing duties required during Jack's absence.

In consideration of Jack's naval experience, combined with the top-notch training that Thorogood was to receive on Padre Island, the elder Kensington had no reservations in assigning this duty to his son.

## The Palms

Jack and the much younger Thorogood took the train west to Texas, arriving in Houston just two days after receiving notification.

There, they chartered private overland transportation to the nearest ferry crossing where they subsequently transferred from stagecoach to boat for the final leg of their journey.

Upon reaching the island, they took up temporary residence at The Palms, a local inn not far from the boat's mooring.

## The Pints

That night, on the eve before instruction in sailing was to begin, Cajun Jack and Thorogood sat alone at the bar in the communal area of The Palms, bonding and discussing their plans over several rounds of rum and beer, resulting in a late arrival the next morning, thereby angering the instructor.

## The Pier

The instructor, an ornery, old sailor many viewed as too old to be instructing, met Jack and Thorogood as they arrived at the pier.

"There'll be no discounts for time missed," he said without introducing himself. "Any objections? I didn't think so. You" —he continued, as he pointed to Thorogood— "grab those ropes and follow me. I understand you're a Greenhorn. That makes our first lesson on knots—the tying kind, not the measuring kind. Any objections? I didn't think so."

## The Prize

Suddenly realizing that he might, indeed, be speaking with the wrong party, he stopped and pointed to the already rigged boat.

"You are the gentlemen here for The Prize, aren't you?"

"The Prize?" Thorogood asked.

"Yes, The Prize," the old sailor continued as he hopped aboard her and pulled back the tarpaulin that covered her name. There, the words, The Prize, were painted aft in a fancy scrolling script.

## The Points of Sail

After revealing her identity to the new owner, and after scolding them for being late, the instruction began. The basics in ropes and knots were covered absolutely too fast for most anyone to remember, but he refused to slow his pace when asked.

Next, he went into great detail regarding the harnessing of wind in relation to the desired bearing of the boat. As he continued talking too fast, sailing terms like 'close hauled,' 'close reach,' 'broad reach,' and 'beam reach' came one after the other, with no room for student distraction, or questions, in between.

He taught them the bowline, the clove hitch, the double loop hitch, the sheet bend, and many lesser-known knots, each usable in their own specialized way. The training lasted all that morning, up until lunchtime, which the old sailor insisted they take at the noon hour each day. And, while he ate, he talked to them, his mouth bulging with food.

## The Privateer

"You'd better pay more attention," he said as he gazed at Thorogood. "Your father's got plans for this vessel."

"The boat's a gift," Thorogood replied.

"A gift to you, maybe, but what you're gonna do with her's gonna be a gift to him."

Thorogood had no idea what the instructor meant, so he looked over to Jack to see if his face was revealing.

You see, Jack had one of those faces unfit for poker. You could see it in his eyes. He simply could not be trusted with confidential matters or secrecy.

"What's he mean, Jack?" Thorogood asked.

"I'd hoped ya daddy'd, tell ya," Jack said in his native Cajun tongue.

"Tell me what?" Thorogood replied.

"She gone be used for smugglin'," Jack replied.

## The Pea Coat

Hearing the news and learning he'd been deceived by his father, Thorogood put on his coat and departed, leaving Jack and the instructor aboard the schooner.

## The Painter

Thorogood returned to the inn, sat down on a barstool, and engaged the bartender in the kind of casual conversation often heard by individuals in this profession. Before long, Thorogood had enlisted the help of the bartender in finding a painter for some touchup work needed on, The Prize.

### The Pre-Dreadnought

He remained at the bar for the rest of that day and into the evening, drinking and talking and thinking. There was no way his new schooner could ever challenge the pre-dreadnoughts that sailed the waters these days. He had no idea what would've caused his father to make such a conclusion.

### The Parallel

And as he continued to drink, he soon realized that his plans for the boat and his father's plans for the boat were no longer compatible, and were, in fact, quite contradictory.

### The Painting

Thorogood returned to the schooner the following morning, where he accepted his scolding 'like a man,' as they used to say, neither revealing to the instructor nor Jack his anger toward his father. He refused to discuss his plans with them regarding the boat. He kept this up throughout the course of his instruction, meeting only after dark with his newly-hired painter, where they worked together in secrecy beneath the tarpaulin.

Approximately six weeks later, after the old man had taught Jack and Thorogood to sail, and after only taking her upon the water twice, the instructor reluctantly, but officially, transferred possession to Thorogood so that they could begin their journey home.

### The Pineapple

As they celebrated above deck that afternoon with drinks of rum and pineapple, Thorogood led them to the aft of the boat. After a very short speech, in which he thanked both Jack and the instructor, he revealed the schooner's new moniker.

"Ona mat… What the hell does that say?" the old man said as he tried to pronounce the boat's name.

"Onomatopoeia," Thorogood replied.

"Who gave you permission to do that?" the instructor asked.

"I don't need permission; she's mine now."

"What do that mean?" Jack added.

Thorogood just laughed and said, "You'll find out soon enough."

## Port O'Connor

The next morning, Jack and Thorogood departed along the Intracoastal Waterway, destined for Port O'Conner, Texas.

## Port Aransas

As they passed Port Aransas, Thorogood, a relatively talkative man at this point in his life, broached the subject regarding his plans for the schooner.

He made Jack aware of his varying ideas for the boat and made it clear that privateering was out of the question. He told Jack that he would never consider using any boat in that way and felt sailing should be for pleasure only.

Jack, responded with just one sentence, "Yo' daddy'll never allow dat."

## The Pelicans

They did not speak until docking later that evening after the many pelicans indigenous to the area had begun to roost.

## The Portside

Below deck, the two men took to their bunks straightaway, with Jack bedding down in the bunk on the starboard side and Thorogood taking the bunk on the port side.

## Port Arthur

The next stop was at Port Arthur, Texas, and much like the day prior, there was very little talk regarding the intended use of the boat.

## Pecan Island

Pecan Island, just west of Vermilion Bay, was next. Once again, the two men spoke very little as the monotony increased with each day.

## Port Fourchon

The next day, they arrived in Port Fourchon, where they remained on the boat for the night, just as they had done every night since leaving South Padre.

## Port Sulphur

The next morning, the pair entered the Mississippi River near Empire and sailed upriver, docking for the night in Port Sulphur, Louisiana.

## Phoenix, Louisiana

Phoenix was next, with only one variation in comparison to the preceding nights. Thorogood, in accordance with his plan and unbeknownst to Jack, had intentionally allowed the boat's provisions to deplete, forcing the men to seek lodging in a nearby inn, where they ate and drank heartily.

And since Thorogood was well aware of Jack's alcoholism, he used the man's sickness against him.

## The Prearranged

Also unknown to Jack was a prearranged agreement Thorogood had made with the man who'd painted and renamed the boat. This is how the plan unfolded.

The painter departed South Padre just after completing his work and arrived in Phoenix days before Jack and Thorogood.

Thorogood, discovering the depleted provisions and feigning surprise regarding the matter, suggested sheltering at an inn for the night, certain that Jack would approve, knowing his fondness for drink.

## Pointe a la Hache

In the early morning hours of the next day, the painter, an experienced sailor himself, was to remove the Onomatopoeia from her mooring and scuttle her downstream near Pointe a la Hache.

## The Peril

For this dangerous and illegal job, Thorogood agreed to pay the painter, in cash, a very handsome but undocumented sum.

## The Ploy

The deception employed in this incident came off without a hitch. The schooner was, indeed, stolen, and easily transported downriver without raising a single sail. The Mississippi's strong current was more than enough to move her swiftly to the predetermined location.

## The People

The citizenry within the vicinity of the boat's mooring were quickly interviewed. Those interviews were recorded and documented, thus making it official. The boat had been stolen by some unknown thief.

## The Piracy

This theft, while not all that uncommon, was rigorously investigated. Nevertheless, the crime would go unsolved, and the location of the boat would remain unknown.

## The Perception

All witnesses interviewed at dockside reported the boat leaving in the early morning hours, roughly four a.m., with one man onboard. All witnesses interviewed at the inn reported both Thorogood and Jack had left the inn at seven am.

Thorogood's ruse was complete. The boat had been stolen by an unknown individual and both Jack and Thorogood were not involved.

## The Paradox

It was at this time that Thorogood wired his father to inform him regarding the theft of the schooner. A response was received immediately. The telegraph operator in New Orleans, an old friend of the elder Mr. Kensington, informed Thorogood of his father's sudden death that morning.

Thorogood was devastated. After struggling to regain his composure, he sent a second wire, addressed only to the telegraph operator. Thorogood asked him to destroy the transcription from the first telegraph and tell no one what he'd learned about the boat. The third and final telegraph addressed to Kensington Manor was sent confirming the successful arrival of the Onomatopoeia at Lake Pontchartrain.

Later that evening at the inn, Jack, who was much wiser and more intelligent than perceived from his outward appearance, asked Thorogood about the boat.

Thorogood explained that the truth hadn't been an option and his ruse had been the only way to prevent his father from privateering. He couldn't reconcile how his father, perceived as righteous and upright by everyone who had known him, could demand the truth from his children while, at the same time, not being truthful with his children.

Jack called this The Paradox of Life when he said, "How can a man who demands the truth, lie?" He added, "How can a man who never lives, die?"

ACT 9

# THE GREAT CHICAGO FIRE

Many months after returning to Kensington Manor, after many months spent searching for the letters he'd sent home during the war, and after many months of pleading for his wife's assistance in locating those letters, Mr. Kensington arrived at a disheartening conclusion.

It was obvious that he'd never be able to locate them without his wife's assistance, and it was equally obvious that her decline, mentally speaking, was now in its advanced stages. Therefore, because he needed someone in whom he could confide, and because his guilt had become too heavy for him to carry alone, Mr. Kensington began to recount some of the events that he'd chronicled in those lost letters, knowing his confessions to her could never jeopardize his freedom.

"Annie," Mr. Kensington began.

"Yes, Thorogood," she replied.

"Have you ever done anything that brought shame upon you or your family?"

"I don't know what you mean, Dear," she answered.

"I didn't think you had. You're just not the type."

Mrs. Kensington did not reply, continuing to gaze upon

their estate from the balcony where they sat, as Mr. Kensington continued, "I've done some terrible things—things that I thought were justified at the time."

Mrs. Kensington had no response as she continued to listen to her husband.

"There's nothing I can do to make amends. I just need to talk to someone."

Mrs. Kensington still said nothing.

"It happened about ten years ago after I'd abandoned the Confederacy. I thought they were after me. I didn't want to be in that regiment, anyway. It felt as if I had no choice," he said as his tone became more desperate. "Why couldn't they just leave me be?"

Mrs. Kensington remained silent, but she did reach and take her husband's hand as he continued to speak.

"I'm a wanted man, you know. Not just by a few. I figure there are many who'd like to get their hands on me."

"Wanted?" Mrs. Kensington inquired.

"Yes."

"By whom?"

"The Army of the Confederate States of America, for one."

"Why would you be wanted by them?"

"I was never missing-in-action or captured by the Union..." he said after pausing and then lowering his head in an outward admission of shame. "I abandoned my post early on and ran."

Mrs. Kensington did not reply, but as she began to release his hand, he held on even more tightly.

"There's more... Much more. I stole money from the Confederacy, and after getting away with it, I guess I just had no hope... No hope of ever returning to the life I'd once known... No hope of being an innocent man."

Mr. Kensington continued, confessing his other crimes to her, and confiding his fear of being caught was both fodder and a catalyst driving him onward, forcing him to commit subsequent crimes, in an effort to silence all witnesses who might be able to testify against him.

"In the summer of 1871, I got wind of a rumor about several men I'd known in the past. It was suggested to me that these men were gonna collect a reward and be given immunity for their crimes by turning state's witness on me… I was terrified, Annie. So, I took a train north to Chicago where the proceedings were scheduled, just to find out if what I'd heard was accurate. You know? I stayed in a boarding house under a false identity and began an investigation… I needed to know the truth. I only wanted to preserve my freedom, and I didn't want to put the Manor in jeopardy. Anyway, I learned rather quickly the rumor was true. This terrified me even more. I thought about turning myself in, but I just couldn't bring myself to do it. I just…"

The usually hardened and stoic Mr. Kensington began to cry. His tears fell openly and unashamedly before the witnessing eyes of his wife. Once he had regained his composure, he continued with his confession.

"After learning the truth, I followed a few of the men for weeks, until I could find out where they were lodging. I finally determined they were sheltered within a government-funded safe house at 137 Dekoven Street. The owner of the house, Catherine O'Leary, had accepted payment on behalf of the men for their room and board. So, on the night of October 8, 1871, while the men slept in Mrs. O'Leary's house, I set fire to her barn and her home, hoping to eliminate these men and prevent their testimony against me. I had no idea the fire would spread."

It was all he could do to finish before breaking down further into a flurry of regret and tears that lasted for nearly forty minutes.

The Great Chicago fire that started in Mrs. O'Leary's barn spread quickly, killing over three-hundred people and consuming over three-square miles of the Greater Chicago area. Over seventeen-thousand wooden balloon-framed structures were completely destroyed. Until now, Mr. Kensington's confession and involvement in this crime have never been documented.

Later that night, the night of Mr. Kensington's admission, Mrs. Kensington helped her husband to bed. His ensuing state of inebriation had prevented him from accomplishing this by himself.

The next morning, as Mr. Kensington recovered from the severe hangover, it was as if Mrs. Kensington had no recollection at all of the confession. She continued to gaze upon him with the same adoration he'd always known.

Two evenings later, as the couple sat upon their balcony admiring their estate, Mrs. Kensington re-engaged her husband regarding the confession from just two days ago.

"Where did you go afterward?" Mrs. Kensington asked in between sips of tea.

"After what?" Mr. Kensington replied.

"After you left Milwaukee."

"Annie, Dear, I've never been to Milwaukee."

"Did your wife travel with you? She was a very lucky woman," Mrs. Kensington said.

"My wife did not accompany me on my travels." He sighed.

Months rolled by as the two spent many evenings in this same way, with Mr. Kensington confessing his sins, and Mrs. Kensington forgetting them almost the moment she'd been told. And periodically, Mr. Kensington would attempt to extract from her the location of those incriminating documents bearing his signature. This disheartening cycle of verbal confession and then not being heard drove Mr. Kensington to seek solace elsewhere. So, late at night, just after seeing his wife off to bed, he recorded, within his journal, many of those incriminating tales that he'd told Mrs. Kensington just hours earlier in the evening.

Modern psychology and religion may suggest that Mr. Kensington's confessions would have a positive effect on both his mind and his soul. However, it provided neither. As he continued to confide in his absentminded wife, his confessions seemed to stir within him an almost undefinable yet realistic turmoil that he hadn't anticipated. He did not feel any better regarding his sins, although he'd asked his maker's forgiveness for them many times. And so began a series of visions and visitations within the darkness of night, in the form of vivid and unforgettable dreams that drove Mr. Kensington further into despair.

The first dream occurred just one week after his confession regarding the Great Chicago Fire.

It all began like this: As Mr. Kensington lay sleeping in his bed, and as the ticking clock on the mantle in his bed chamber approached two am, the door to his room opened slightly. A black feline entered the room, slowly walking toward him. In the dream, Mr. Kensington witnessed these events as a spectator and even saw his own likeness still sleeping undisturbed in his bed. As the cat neared the bed, he leaped over the footboard and onto the bed with a single bound, where he proceeded to walk the length of the bed atop the sleeping Mr. Kensington, who remained undisturbed. The tag dangling from the collar around the cat's neck simply read, 'TOM.'

After the initial onset of this dream, it recurred nightly, without variation, for just over two months. At that point, the dream increased in length, while retaining all aspects of the previous dream which had occurred nightly for the last sixty-two days.

On the sixty-third occurrence of this dream, the cat jumped onto the bed, just as before. However, this time, upon reaching the area where Mr. Kensington's head should be, the cat learned the body within the bed had been decapitated. The cat didn't look surprised, but rather, as if its sole intention was to make the spectator, who was also Mr. Kensington, aware of the decapitation. The headless body within the bed wore a Confederate uniform bearing a major's insignia. The tag on the collar around the cat's neck now had additional verbiage. Underneath the word 'TOM' were the words, 'P.G.T. Beauregard.'

The haunting and unsettling dream consumed Mr. Kensington's thoughts during that time, effectively replacing his obsession with the missing letters. He talked to his wife about the dream every day, searching for some semblance of meaning.

Finally reaching a breaking point, Mr. Kensington sought information at 1113 Chartres Street in the French Quarter, home of Confederate General Pierre Gustave Toutant Beauregard. Surprisingly, at this address, he found a much more modest dwelling than his own. Reluctant to introduce himself to the servants who greeted him, he refused to give his name. He was informed of the general's absence and asked to return at a future date if he still wished to speak with the general. Unwilling to accept those terms, Mr. Kensington engaged Henri Babineux, butler to General Beauregard.

"Can you tell me where I can find the general?" Mr. Kensington asked.

"I don't discuss the general's business, Sir," Henri replied.

"It's very important I speak with the general," Mr. Kensington persisted.

"As I've told you, Sir, the general is indisposed at the moment. Are you acquainted with the general, Sir?"

"I've never been formally introduced, but I have to speak with him."

"I suggest you write the general a letter. If you wish, I can have it wired to him at once."

Mr. Kensington did not immediately respond, knowing the general might not consider his line of questions important.

"Maybe you can help me," Mr. Kensington said after rethinking the situation.

"Sir, as I've told you, I do not discuss the general's business."

"This matter is not business-related," Mr. Kensington explained. "It's about the general's cat."

"The general has no pets, Sir. If you've found an animal, it does not belong to General Beauregard."

"The tag bears the General's name," Mr. Kensington argued.

"That's not possible, Sir. As I've already told you, the general has no pets," Henri said as he traversed the foyer where the men were standing and opened the front door.

"Are you sure? I think his name is Tom."

The expression on Henri's face changed abruptly as if he'd seen a ghost, and he closed the door before Mr. Kensington could exit.

"What color is this cat, Sir?" Henri asked.

"He's black and quite large, for a cat, that is."

"I can't see how this is possible," Henri exclaimed as he immediately sat down upon the winged chair in the entryway. "There was a time, some years ago, when the general had a pet cat named Tom. He was, indeed, black, and very large, like you mentioned. In 1864, this cat was killed by enemy fire during a battle in Georgia. The general was deeply affected by this event. He no longer has pets. You say you've found this cat?"

At this point, Mr. Kensington did not have a proper response. He had not found the cat—not literally. So, as he and Henri stood in the foyer near the door, the gathering silence became awkward.

"Sir?" Henri prompted.

Mr. Kensington did not respond; his silence continued to linger. Then he remembered a phrase he'd recently read from a book of proverbs and idioms: 'Curiosity killed the cat."

Suddenly plagued by second thoughts, Mr. Kensington turned and exited General Beauregard's home without speaking further to the butler who'd greeted him.

While walking home that day, Mr. Kensington decided that any questions he had regarding his recurring dream of TOM and General Beauregard would just have to remain unanswered. Attempting to satisfy his curiosity by breaching this topic with the general might equate to stirring a hornet's nest. Rather than 'kill the cat,' it might 'kill the Bull.'

The recurring dream finally stopped when Mr. Kensington decided to refrain from dwelling upon it during waking hours. It was replaced by a more unusual and more vivid dream about mathematics.

# Pythagorean Theorem

You may be wondering, how does mathematics play a role in Mr. Kensington's obsessions, his death, and the subsequent investigation into his death?

## **The Preamble**

My response to you is that everything in our lives relates to mathematics. For instance, in literature, the chapters and pages are numbered sequentially. Poetry, like haiku, consists of seventeen syllables and three lines. Astronomy's great distances are measured in light years, and formally unknown planetary objects, such as Neptune, discovered in 1846, became known through mathematical observation. In music, measures, beats, and crescendos are mathematically patternistic. The strategies, provisionings, and overall successes of wars are all about the numbers. And science? Well, science speaks for itself.

I could go on with nearly infinite examples, but in deference to time and space, I'll draw this conclusion. Math is the foundation upon which all things are built, and it's upon this foundation that we must strive to use mathematics' many formulas and theories to our advantage in efforts to conquer the challenges we encounter. In doing so, you'll find it pertinent to match the correct formula or theorem to the problem at hand. For this problem, the murder of Thorogood Kensington, I recommend one of those mathematical theorems—specifically, the Pythagorean Theorem.

## <u>Pythagoras</u>

Pythagoras, a self-proclaimed 'lover of wisdom,' was a Greek philosopher and mathematician who lived during the pre-Socratic era. As the son of a wealthy merchant, Pythagoras was well-educated, obtaining his knowledge in Greece, India, and Egypt. He is well-known for his work in philosophy and is attributed as an influence on subsequent Greek philosophers, Plato and Aristotle. He is also well-known for his many contributions to mathematics, including the Theory of Proportions, Pythagorean Tuning, a mathematical system used for tuning musical instruments, and most famously, The Pythagorean Theorem.

## <u>Pythagoras' Theorem</u>

In simplified terms, the Pythagorean Theorem is used to calculate the length of the hypotenuse of a right triangle. In short, $a^2+b^2=c^2$.

## <u>The Papers</u>

There's no mistaking the fact that Mr. Kensington developed a burning interest in mathematics that originated in 1881 and lasted until his death. The many documents, journals, and papers found in the drawers of his desk that day substantiated this as an evidentiary fact. The troves of investigators who descended on Kensington Manor that day recorded, within casework files, no less than three-hundred individual papers, signed by Mr. Kensington himself, showing variants and attempted proofs of Pythagoras' Theorem. However, the initial investigators saw no relevance between the papers and Mr. Kensington's death. I thought the quantity of papers related to this subject was too great to ignore.

## The Perpendicular Lines

Many hand-drawn intersecting lines had been produced in repeated attempts to create graph papers for future work.

## The Points and Plotting

Some of these papers had points already plotted, suggesting the plotter, somehow, attempted to prove the theorem once more before failing. These papers were neither torn nor crumbled, but rather, indexed chronologically by date and time, and signed by the plotter.

## The Protractor

A metal, handmade protractor was also found with the aforementioned paperwork. This mathematical instrument was engraved with the initials J.A.G.

## The Parallelogram

Many parallelograms had been drawn and graphed to precision, then bisected, forming multiple triangles, with each one relating to an adjacent handwritten formula.

## The Pencil

All of these papers were in Mr. Kensington's hand, written in pencil, and all appeared to be renderings of the Pythagorean Theorem.

## The Protagonist

In early 1862, just after Mr. Kensington had been recruited into the Pointe Coupee artillery regiment, there was another young man within the opposing ranks, working feverishly, recruiting young men into the newly-formed 42nd Cavalry Regiment of Ohio. This young man and future President was James Garfield.

## Paintsville, Kentucky

That January, after organizing his regiment, and subsequent to their training, Garfield marched his men to Paintsville, Kentucky. There, they engaged the enemy at the Battle of Middle Creek. This battle, led by Garfield, was instrumental and set the stage for the future control of eastern Kentucky by Union forces.

## Promotion

Afterward, Garfield and his troops moved to Prestonsburg for reprovisioning, and as a result of his successes on the battlefield, Garfield was promoted to brigadier general.

## Pound Gap

Garfield's next commanding engagement occurred at Pound Gap. This skirmish would prove vital in forcing remaining Confederate troops to vacate Kentucky; they retreated into Virginia. Garfield now controlled the 20th Brigade of the Army of Ohio. Afterward, Garfield suffered a minor setback by contracting jaundice, which, in turn, forced his removal from the battlefield and his return to Washington.

In Washington, Garfield would prove himself again by successfully serving as Chief of Staff to Major General William S. Rosecrans, and ultimately being elected 20th President of the United States in 1881.

## The President

President Garfield, an abolitionist who supported the Gold Standard, was known for many progressive policies including a universal, federally-funded education system for all Americans, and reformation of civil rights. Most of Garfield's policies were well-received. However, there were some of his policies that caused strife and resentment amongst his opponents and his constituents.

## The Post Office Purge

Just after his election, Garfield became aware of wide-reaching corruption within the Post Office of the United States. On his order, the corruption was investigated and rooted out, resulting in many individuals, both Republican and Democratic, becoming ensnared.

## Pendleton Civil Service Reform Act

This investigation, and the fallout from it, would eventually lead to the Pendleton Civil Service Reform Act, which states that civil servants must be hired based upon their knowledge and ability, as determined by a civil service test, rather than by the former method of appointment—cronyism. These radical changes in governmental policy were not popular and could be the catalyst that led to Garfield's subsequent assassination just six months after being inaugurated.

## The Pistol

On July 2, 1881, Charles Giteau, feeling that Garfield owed him a governmental appointment, and upset about Garfield's policies, shot President Garfield twice, from behind, at the Baltimore and

Potomac Railroad Station. Giteau's weapon of choice was a .44 caliber British Bulldog revolver that he'd purchased just weeks before the killing with money he claimed had been lent to him by George Maynard, a relative. Garfield died on September 19th from an infection that developed after the shooting. Giteau was later hung after his conviction on the charge of murder.

## The Persistent

It was close to the time of President Garfield's assassination, during the summer of 1881, that Mr. Kensington's dreams changed from cat to math. It was also at this time, Thorogood developed his obsession with formulas and theorems and began his attempts at proving those theorems within his journal.

## The Pythagorean Theorem

Mr. Kensington was an intelligent man, educated at Louisiana State Seminary of Learning and Military Academy. Early on, he'd adopted and applied to his life the motto, 'knowledge is power,' taken from Sir Francis Bacon's book, Meditationes Sacrae. It was, indeed, this motto and his thirst for knowledge that led to his successes in life. It was also this motto that would lead to his downfall.

Realizing he'd played a part in the death of James Garfield was more than he could accept. Thus began his obsession. Night after night, he sat behind his desk, plotting and drawing, grafting then formulating, measuring then penciling, but to no avail. He'd learned through the many published articles since Garfield's assassination that the President was a highly intelligent man, and in 1876, he had published proof of Pythagorean's Theorem in the New England Journal of Education. Knowing that 'knowledge is power,' Mr. Kensington set out to prove the theorem on his own.

This would also prove his equality with James Garfield, and in some way, this proof might relieve the guilt he felt over Garfield's assassination. However, no matter how many times he tried, he failed.

About six months before this obsession had begun, and just days after Garfield's election, a visitor had come to the door at Kensington Manor. This visitor was unlike the many other parties who had knocked on the manor house door over the years. This man was known to Mr. Kensington, had a history with Kensington Manor, and brought news of encouragement to their door.

The forty-year-old man had introduced himself as Charles Julius Guiteau, current lawyer and political activist, and former stable hand at Kensington Manor from 1851 to 1853.

Mr. Kensington had not seen this person in many years, but memories of the boy returned as if they had occurred only yesterday. After their seemingly happy reacquaintance, Charles had been enthusiastically welcomed inside and invited to sup that evening with both Mr. and Mrs. Kensington.

Later that evening, Mr. Kensington had fondly recalled the interaction he'd witnessed years earlier between the visitor, who was approximately ten years of age at that time, and his beloved steed. "Charles, I remember well your work ethic, and how you wanted to spend all of your time in the stable. I'm not sure which of us loved the animal more," Mr. Kensington had said as they raised glass after glass of cabernet.

"He was your steed, Sir. You loved him most, but I could argue that he preferred me over you."

Mr. Kensington had been taken aback by such an arrogant statement until he heard the explanation.

"You just rode him, while I fed him, brushed him, and cared for him."

Mr. Kensington had laughed. "Ah, yes, Charles. I see, and you are correct."

Then, after a brief diversion of eating and drinking, Mr. Kensington had asked, "So, tell me, Charles, what brings you to Kensington Manor after all these years?"

"Well, Sir, I'm sure I don't have to inform you about the current political climate in our nation's capital. The newly-elected President does not and will not promote policies that reflect our mutual interests. As you know, my legal experience, and my desire to help men just like you, has led me to my new calling."

Then as Charles had raised his glass of wine he'd announced, "I want to seek public office in Washington, to represent people just like you and me, and to return to us what is rightfully ours."

This announcement, if only briefly, had reignited the gleam in Mr. Kensington's eyes as he'd confirmed his agreement by raising his glass to a toast and saying, "Here, here!"

"You know, Mr. Kensington, for a nominal campaign contribution, you could be instrumental in my efforts in Washington. Not to mention, you would have priority access to legal representation, when needed."

Mr. Kensington, without hesitation, had donated to the campaign fund of Charles Julius Giteau in the amount of fifteen dollars.

Six months later, Mr. Kensington would regret this contribution and embark on his lengthy and unsuccessful journey attempting to prove the Pythagorean Theorem.

During Mr. Kensington's preoccupation with this mathematical formula, a distance began to grow between him and his wife. The many hours they'd once spent together walking the plantation, taking high-tea together on the balcony, or just enjoying a stolen moment alone, began to dwindle into non-existence. The neglect from her once-loving husband became too much for any woman to endure. Desiring reconciliation, Mrs. Kensington began to question her husband, with her questions increasing in quantity and volume, while his answers decreased in quantity and volume. Mr. Kensington was also in search of answers. His only respite from his mathematical effort was the monthly weekend away—when he told his wife he was sailing on his boat.

"Where are you going?" Mrs. Kensington asked him one day.

"Sailing."

"Don't you ever tire of that boat?"

Mr. Kensington ignored her as he prepared his travel bag for another overnight trip.

"Thorogood, are you listening to me?" Mrs. Kensington asked.

He seemed not to notice her inquiry and continued to pack his suitcase.

No matter how much time Mr. Kensington spent 'sailing,' it did not appear to help. He would only exchange one obsession for another.

## ACT 11

# DISHONESTY, DEMENTIA OR DELIRIUM

As my investigation continued, I delved deeper into the journal and the other documents I'd found in Mr. Kensington's study. The volume of paperwork contained within the desk was staggering. I wasn't sure I could review all the documents without help and I wondered if I should seek assistance. This self-doubt—my old, familiar nemesis—had returned, and upon examining the journal further, I found the entries had been made by two different hands. The handwriting before the date of Mr. Kensington's death matched the handwriting on the many mathematical documents. The handwriting on the entries after the date of his death had been made by another person. The last entry in the journal, the only entry having a signature, was signed simply, 'Jack.'

This journal and the many other documents in the desk resulted in a series of curve balls thrown in my direction, heightening my suspicion of some individuals while lowering my suspicion of others. My investigation into the history of Kensington Manor and Mr. Kensington's death, along with my investigation into the current oddities within the house, began to consume me.

Some months after taking up residence at Kensington Manor, Molly, the one Mr. Standish introduced to me as Penelope, began acting in a strange manner, similar to the behavior being expressed by the lady of the house.

She became quick to anger, rude, and at times, quite nasty to everyone in the house. Complaints were relayed to me by almost everyone there, except for one male of dubious origins and motivations. Unsurprisingly, Mr. Standish made no comments on her behavior.

Just ten days after the onset of this change in her character, Penelope, or Molly, or whatever-you-want-to-call-her, fled the house, never to be seen again by any of us. Within hours of her departure, Mr. Standish followed suit by leaving the house without a single word of warning. Prior to their departure, my suspicions of both of them were on an upward trajectory. Now, after reevaluating these events, I decided they'd probably had a lover's quarrel.

Word of vacancies must travel fast within the realm of boarders and boarding houses, because less than one week later, a newcomer arrived at our door, appearing hungry and disheveled, only to be welcomed with open arms by Mrs. Kensington. I did not understand this immediate welcoming of a new boarder. It hadn't been long ago that Mrs. Kensington had invited all of us to vacate the premises, which we had successfully delayed through various tactics. Seeing an opportunity to lengthen our residency at Kensington Manor, I suggested to the others that we attempt to quell the tension left in the house by Molly and Mr. Standish by making every attempt to get along with this new girl. Thus, we all decided to join Mrs. Kensington in welcoming our newest boarder, Pandora, into our home with open arms.

The next day, it happened again. It was as if we'd run an advertisement in the local classifieds. This local fellow, who called himself Beauregard, appeared at the door of Kensington Manor just after lunch, penniless and hungry. Once again, Mrs. Kensington welcomed him, no questions asked, and while I was not opposed to the presence of new boarders, I felt she should, at least, vet them before extending them room and board.

That evening, I suppose because of the newcomers, I found an announcement on the knob of my door.

```
        Greetings from 113 Rue Cheshire
              The Kensingtons
 do hereby request your presence at their home
     for a formal gala to begin at 8:00 pm on
         Sunday, December 10th, 1881
-----------------------------------------------

       ------------------------------
```

The seven of us long-term boarders took our usual places in the grand dining hall, leaving vacant the two places formerly occupied by Mr. Standish and Molly. The two newcomers filled those spots without asking or being instructed by me or Mrs. Kensington. Just as she'd done at our many other galas, Mrs. Kensington wheeled around, serving us one by one, until arriving where Mr. Standish normally sat, which was just beside Molly, or Penelope, depending on how you remember her.

Anyway, just as Mrs. Kensington began to serve Beauregard she said, "There you are, Mr. Standish. I know how you like this."

Mrs. Kensington was referring to the selected entree served that evening, which was, indeed, favored by Mr. Standish. As she moved on to Penelope she said, "I know you favor this dish too, Molly."

*This evening is off to a bizarre start*, I thought.

She hadn't noticed the two newcomers, Pandora and Beauregard, and in fact, had mistaken them for the two individuals who'd recently departed our house under questionable circumstances. In fairness, there were some similarities between our new roommates and the previous ones, like hair color, eyes, and maybe size. Still, I worried Mrs. Kensington was losing touch with reality. Or maybe it was something else. Apparently, she'd forgotten the pending evictions, as well.

I was puzzled, to say the least.

After the meal, we all adjourned to the theater for a little music, as was customary at Kensington Manor. This time, things didn't go as planned. As always, Mrs. Kensington placed the disc upon the turntable and wound the Victrola. The expected rotation of the turntable failed to happen, reducing the lady of the house to tears, and prematurely ending our otherwise pleasant evening.

Later, as I made my nightly trip to relieve myself, I stopped by Mrs. Kensington's closed door, as the light underneath drew my attention. Carefully placing an ear near the keyhole, I could discern a conversation already in progress between the widow and her dead husband.

## **Dishonesty**

As the monologue progressed, I learned that dear Mrs. Kensington was not being as honest with me as I'd thought. I overheard her confessions to the late Mr. Kensington regarding members of our household whom she held in low regard. She mentioned a 'her' and a 'him,' as if referring to one male and one female, but to whom was she referring? I could not determine who she meant from the arbitrary terms she used. This left me wondering if I were the 'him' in her conversation. In her current state of mind, I wasn't sure if even she didn't know.

Prior to her desire to evict, she'd told me many times that everyone within our house pleased her and brought joy and purpose to her life. Now, she was telling Mr. Kensington the near opposite. Evidently, two of her nine boarders were not welcome in her home, but she didn't know how to handle the matter diplomatically. They concluded, or rather, she concluded this discussion by agreeing with the advice given her by her husband. Obviously, this remained a mystery to me.

## Dementia

The next day, as I descended the staircase, I sensed the presence of additional people in our home. When I reached the parlor, I found Mrs. Kensington lying on her favorite settee lounge, attended by her friend and personal physician, Dr. Condos Poirot and his nurse.

"There, there. Just drink this," he said as he urged her to finish the cup of tea he'd just brewed.

Dr. Condos Poirot graduated from the Medical College of the State of South Carolina in Charleston, receiving his Doctorate in Medicine in 1847. He went on to excel in the field of botany, where his research was published in the *Southern Journal of Medicine and Pharmacy*. After serving the Confederacy as a surgeon on the battlefield, he returned to private practice, where he became personal physician to the owners and residents of Kensington Manor. Dr. Poirot favored holistic and natural remedies, often using his expertise in botany to his patient's advantage by recommending cures and treatments derived from the many indigenous plants available in any given area.

As I stood, unacknowledged, some twenty feet from this suspicious duo hovering over their patient, I overheard their discussion regarding Mrs. Kensington's condition and the prescribed treatment to be administered by the nurse.

"I'm afraid Mrs. Kensington is suffering from the early stages of dementia," Dr. Poirot explained. "She needs someone here who can watch over her; someone who can see that she takes her medicine daily. Are you prepared to serve her in this manner?" he asked the nurse.

Dr. Poirot's nurse confirmed her willingness to stay at Kensington Manor to oversee Mrs. Kensington's medicinal regimen. Afterward, he instructed his nurse on brewing the various teas that he'd prescribed as treatment. I watched, still unnoticed, trying my best to determine what ingredients were being used.

The next morning, circumstances changed once again. Mrs. Kensington seemed at odds with all nine of us boarding in her home.

"Mr. Peabody," she said, "I thought you had left with the others."

*Others? What others?* I thought to myself. Was she referring to Mr. Standish and Molly? I didn't exactly know to whom she was referring.

"My patience is at an end, Mr. Peabody. You have twenty-four hours, or I shall pursue legal action."

I thought it best not to reply so that she could not hold my response against me, so I just left her there alone on her settee.

The next morning, after a somewhat sleepless night, I felt it important to call an unscheduled tenant meeting so that we might discuss our options.

I called the meeting to order and introduced the first topic of discussion, forgetting to check the suggestion box altogether. I informed my fellow housemates of Mrs. Kensington's medical diagnosis and her renewed desire for us to vacate the property. I noticed Beauregard rolling his eyes at the first order of business, which irritated me somewhat. He seemed unconcerned regarding his impending homelessness. Josephine, Kitty, and Rose huddled together, uninterested in the topic as well. Their body language seemed to suggest they were gossiping about Pandora, the new girl. She paid them no attention as she sat alone, observing the proceedings. Mr. and Mrs. O'Keefe had recently become closer to Ginger, and the three were now inseparable, and all were unshaken by the news. As for me, Jasper Peabody, I had no idea what to do or how to change Mrs. Kensington's mind.

Two nights later, fastened to my door, was the following notice:

```
        Greetings from 113 Rue Cheshire
                The Kensingtons
   do hereby request your presence at their home
       for a formal gala to begin at 8:00 pm on
             Sunday, December 10th, 1881
----------------------------------------------------

         ---------------------------------
```

That evening, we gathered around the table that had been decorated with balloons and streamers of purple, green, and gold. As always, our hostess Mrs. Kensington rolled from place setting to place setting, serving each of us individually. After filling all nine bowls, she announced with enthusiasm, "Happy Mardi Gras!"

We all just stared at her, some of us with food still in our mouths. By this point, I was flabbergasted. Mardi Gras is traditionally celebrated in  February or March; this was August 24th.

I was worried about her. The constant mood swings—wanting us to leave one minute, then celebrating with us, the next. I was running out of theories on Mrs. Kensington and decided that dishonesty had no bearing on her behavior. Her condition must be just as her physician had diagnosed. She must, indeed, be afflicted with dementia.

After the meal, Mrs. Kensington gathered us around the Victrola for the customary evening music. Upon finding her turntable out-of-order, Mrs. Kensington, the once graceful hostess, experienced what I can only define as a nervous breakdown. She seemed to be unaware that the machine was broken. I'd heard her place a call to the repairman myself. She then accused each of us, in succession, of breaking the machine, while there was no proof that any of us were actually responsible for the damage. Her nurse, who'd already retired for the evening, was awakened, due to Mrs. Kensington's outburst, and subsequently came to her patient's aid, at which point, she chased us from the room. I was terrified.

The next morning, I could hear a man's voice downstairs conversing with Mrs. Kensington's nurse. He was invited into the house and led straightaway to the theater where he was shown the broken Victrola. The simple repair was completed within thirty minutes.

Moments later, Dr. Poirot arrived at our door. I suppose he'd been notified of Mrs. Kensington's outburst the night before. I further supposed he was there to check on the current status of her health.

I paid particular attention to the doctor and his nurse during this visit and learned more about them and the patient. Mrs. Kensington's diagnosis of dementia was changed from early-stage to late-stage. This seemed rather quick to me. After all, it had only been days since her original diagnosis, and this change in her status aroused my suspicion.

In addition, I heard the nurse ask the doctor if Mrs. Kensington's desire to rid the house of us boarders was accurate. He responded by confirming the desire and also asked if she could assist with the evictions. She half-heartedly agreed to assist in the endeavor.

This new information called for yet another impromptu meeting of the tenants.

I called this last-minute meeting to order after peeking into the suggestion box. There were no suggestions, so I promptly informed the others of what I had learned. This time, I could tell that most of the others were concerned with the matter, just by the expressions on their faces. As for their opinions on Mrs. Kensington's health, that issue was met with mixed emotions.

Josephine, Kitty, and Rose maintained their solidarity when expressing their thoughts on the matter. They believed I was mistaken and there was no cause to worry. Meanwhile, Beauregard had recently become more familiar with Ginger and the two of them, along with the O'Keefes, shared the same opinion—there was no cause to be alarmed. Pandora, still the new girl, was the only holdout. I know this due to her unwillingness to agree with the others. She simply maintained a position of neutrality on the topic, which suggested to me that the news I'd shared with them should, at the very least, be investigated further.

The next day, after I'd resigned myself to the possibility that eviction was imminent, I found the following announcement awaiting me at my door.

```
        Greetings from 113 Rue Cheshire
               The Kensingtons
   do hereby request your presence at their home
      for a formal gala to begin at 8:00 pm on
           Sunday, December 10th, 1881
--------------------------------------------------------

        ----------------------------------
```

I entered the grand dining hall to find all of my housemates already at their assigned places. I was the last to arrive. After a moment of slight embarrassment, fearing that I'd lost track of time, my level of embarrassment became even further elevated.

"Happy Birthday, Mr. Peabody!" Mrs. Kensington shouted as she rushed over and placed a party hat on my head by stretching the rubber band fastener under my chin.

I didn't know what to say. No one had ever thrown a party in my honor—neither a birthday party nor any other type of party. So I said nothing and accepted the unexpected accolade without reservation.

This surprise event only raised my suspicions, however, because, although I did not have the heart to tell her, my birthday wasn't for another seven months.

Next, my hostess and widow of nearly thirty years, the dear Mrs. Kensington belted out her rendition of 'Happy Birthday in my honor, or so I assumed.

```
            "Happy Birthday to you.
            Happy Birthday to you.
        Happy Birthday, Mr. Kensington.
            Happy Birthday to you."
```

At first, I thought maybe she was just confused, but what happened next heightened my concern, and the concerns of my previously unconcerned housemates.

"Here you are, Thorogood, just what you asked for."

And with that, Mrs. Kensington placed a potted plant before me on the tabletop. It was adorned with a single red ribbon tied around the base to which a card had been affixed with a straight pin.

"Well, go ahead, Mr. Kensington, read your card," she suggested.

I was shocked, and by this time, I suspected it was no longer just her medical diagnosis that was affecting her memory. I believed the others felt the same way, as they stared in disbelief. Before I could examine the card, Mrs. Kensington's nurse burst onto the scene, forcing all of us to retreat to the seclusion of our rooms amidst a verbal scolding for encouraging the lady of the house to overexert herself.

The very next morning, Dr. Poirot was at the house, assisting Mrs. Kensington as she lay upon the chase lounge in the parlor. It was at this time, I overheard the following exchange.

"How are we feeling today, Mrs. Kensington?" Dr. Poirot asked.

"I feel better in the early morning, just after waking, Doctor," Mrs. Kensington replied.

"Any episodes since my last visit?" the doctor asked as he turned toward the nurse.

## Delirium

"Yes, Doctor. Mrs. Kensington seems to experience bouts of delirium and delusion which occur approximately every other evening.

"Can you further define this delirium?" the doctor asked.

"She has trouble recalling things that occurred just moments prior, and sometimes forgets my name. It's as if she's living in the past, at times. Then, by morning, the delusion has usually left her."

"That's the first sign of someone in her condition," the doctor replied.

"She overwound her Victrola but doesn't remember doing it at all. She accused me and Mr. Peabody of the damage," the nurse added.

"Has it been repaired? I know of Mrs. Kensington's fondness for music, and the sound is good for her continued rehabilitation."

"Yes, doctor, it has been repaired."

"You are doing fine, Mrs. Kensington. You are on your way to a speedy recovery," the doctor added as he bade farewell to the lady of the house, and subsequently, consulted the nurse in privacy, or so they thought.

"There's not much more we can do for her. Just continue to comfort her and make sure she continues with the tea. It will soothe her senses and help her sleep."

She smiled her understanding, one of the first times I'd seen her do that. I couldn't shake the feeling there was something insincere about it. It didn't reach her eyes, and not to brag or anything, but I have a sense about people.

"Yes, doctor," she replied. "You can count on me."

# THE RECONSTRUCTION

### Retrospect

After Mr. Kensington's return to Kensington Manor in 1881, after the assassination of President Garfield, and after Mr. Kensington disposed of his mathematical obsession, he embarked on an interim period of clearer thinking, which revitalized the manor house and plantation. You might say, he found a new obsession.

### Rethinking

After years of worrying about his past, the crimes he'd committed in the past, and his possible capture and prosecution regarding those crimes, Thorogood Kensington changed his paradigm on these matters, placing them and their possible consequences behind him.

### Revitalization

Because of this new frame of mind, Kensington Manor began to flourish. Many paid workers were hired, the soil was tilled, crops were planted, and its colorful past began to return when those crops brought forth an abundant harvest. Profitability soon followed as the corn, cotton, and tobacco were harvested, then sold. This period of revitalization could be seen all around the estate. Kensington Manor's successful period of rebirth could be seen on the facade of the manor house, as well, after exterior remodeling was complete. Many of the formerly standing outbuildings were reconstructed to their original specifications. The beautiful colors of the rainbow that had existed in the distant past returned, arching over the acreage known as Kensington Manor, and ending in the grand dining hall of the manor house.

## **<u>Rejuvenation</u>**

Subsequently, Kensington Manor was abuzz with a flurry of daily activities, all necessary to maintain the massive and interdependent epicenter, busy as a beehive, you might say. The question now being asked by one person after another around Kensington Manor was, how did such a recently destitute man afford the large overhead of operating the plantation? These questions all pointed back to Mr. Kensington's past, rejuvenating the old mystery of Schrodinger's Gold. If Mr. Kensington had hoarded or stolen large amounts of money and gold, he was no longer worried about its secrecy. He spent lavishly, sparing no expense, to restore the former glory of Kensington Manor.

## **<u>Restoration</u>**

Most days, following Kensington Manor's restoration, you could find the man of the house, Thorogood Kensington, strolling the grounds of his plantation or atop his favorite horse, loping here and galloping there, enjoying the expansiveness of his estate.

On other days, usually on the third Saturday and Sunday of

each month, when Mrs. Kensington was asked about his where-abouts she replied, "He's on the Onomatopoeia."

This is what she truly believed, and no one ever questioned her response, until that fateful day…

It was on a Sunday—after he'd already departed to go 'sailing on the Onomatopoeia,' otherwise known as visiting his half-sister in the French Quarter—that Mr. Kensington was recognized by one of the many hands who regularly worked his plantation while dining in public with his half-sister. You can imagine what happened next.

The farmhand said nothing to Mrs. Kensington, and Mr. Kensington did not realize he'd been seen.

However, several days later, after the gossip had made its rounds at Kensington Manor, Mrs. Kensington broached the subject to her husband.

"Did you enjoy your weekend with her, Thorogood?" she asked.

"Yes, dear, I had a wonderful time," Mr. Kensington replied.

"Do you love her?"

"I've loved her since first sight," Mr. Kensington replied.

## **Regret**

This response caused Mrs. Kensington to erupt into tears as she ran up the stairs, entered her bedroom, and locked the door, halting Mr. Kensington's pursuit in the hall just outside the door as he pleaded for an explanation. All of this, based upon a misunderstanding, born from dishonesty.

As you already know, the Onomatopoeia was at the bottom of the Mississippi, but Mrs. Kensington didn't know that. As far as she knew, Mr. Kensington had been sailing the waters of Lake Pontchartrain on his schooner for years now. So how did this misunderstanding originate?

### Remorse

Well, Mr. Kensington learned of his father's sudden death after he had enacted his plan to prevent his father from smuggling and privateering via the Onomatopoeia. Embarrassed by his rash actions, racked by regret and shame, he decided to keep the fate of the schooner secret from those at Kensington Manor. If only he had waited—the boat would not be sunk, his father could not coerce him into privateering upon her, and the despair, guilt, and shame he felt regarding her demise would not exist. Rather than explain her sinking to his family and those who respected him, he lied.

The truth about lies is that they are never singular. They are always plural, for as each lie originates, there are inevitably others that follow to maintain the ruse. It was these subsequent lies that led to this misunderstanding between husband and wife.

The 'her' to whom Mrs. Kensington was referring was the woman seen with her husband, while the 'her' to whom Mr. Kensington was referring was his boat. This misunderstanding would last for months, resulting in a wedge driven between Mr. and Mrs. Kensington. Once the truth was uncovered, and the wedge removed, the hole that remained would swallow all future trust between husband and wife. This was compounded when Mrs. Kensington learned of Mr. Kensington's half-sister and the money he'd been giving her to survive.

Once the trust had been broken, Mr. and Mrs. Kensington rarely spoke to one another directly. Their communication with each other was reduced to a childish and petty method wherein each of them chose a personal liaison. Mrs. Kensington selected her friend and personal physician, Dr. Condos Poirot to communicate with her husband on her behalf. Mr. Kensington's chosen messenger was Cajun Jack, former captain of the Onomatopoeia and confidante.

Months passed, and the tension between husband and wife did not improve. In fact, it seemed to worsen. This caused both messengers to consult with one another in an attempt to reconcile the formerly, happily married couple.

Cajun Jack, a quiet man by nature, was uncomfortable with his new assignment and attempted to withdraw on numerous occasions. Reluctantly, he would be compelled to return by Mr. Kensington's promises of a raise in pay. Dr. Poirot, on the other hand, seemed enthusiastic about the circumstances and welcomed the job of 'messenger' to the lady of the house with fervor. This enthusiasm prompted Mrs. Kensington to begin calling the doctor by the pet name of Mercury. He was now, in many ways, viewed by her, not only as a messenger but also as a god, due to his numerous successes in nursing her back to good health. This arrangement would last until Mr. Kensington's death.

In addition to acquiring the services of Dr. Poirot, Mrs. Kensington hired Monks Sterning as her personal valet. This young man served Mrs. Kensington as footman, if you will. Basically, his function was to handle menial tasks that were beneath Dr. Poirot's station. Gweneth Archer was also placed under Mrs. Kensington's employ, acting as her lady-in-waiting, at her beck and call at a moment's notice.

Mr. Kensington hired just one personal assistant, in addition to Jack. This young man's name was Alphonso Morie, and his primary duty was to keep Mr. Kensington's horse in prime condition. Mr. Kensington also hired two farmhands—Able Forester and his assistant, a Mr. Collinsword, both with logging experience—in an attempt to harvest one of the remaining assets available to him.

As a result of this division at the highest level of management at Kensington Manor, changes affecting numerous staff members were enacted. Employees who had been hired by Mrs. Kensington, yet reported to Mr. Kensington, were fired and replaced by others vetted by the man of the house. Employees who had been hired by Mr. Kensington, yet reported to Mrs. Kensington, were also fired, and replaced by others vetted by the lady of the house. This shake-up in personnel caused discord and hurt feelings amongst those fired and amongst many of those who remained. In fact, both Mr. Kensington's and Mrs. Kensington's life and well-being were threatened by numerous individuals formerly in their employ. However, these threats did not affect policy, and those firings were not reversed.

## Reverted

How was the man of the house supposed to know that the revitalization of his manor home would be so short-lived, beginning with that one singular non-truth about the schooner? How could he have realized that one lie would set into motion a plan which would redirect the driving of that proverbial 'final nail' away from the walls of Kensington Manor and straight to his coffin?

Had Mr. Kensington known his fate, and the fate of his beloved manor, maybe he would have been more receptive to reconciliation. Hindsight is twenty-twenty, they say, but foresight is worth its weight in gold. It's the lack of foresight that would be Mr. Kensington's ultimate downfall.

Stubbornness seems to creep into all marriages at some point, but not like theirs. The physical separation between Mr. and Mrs. Kensington soon grew wider and would result in the two not seeing one another, in the flesh, for days. Days soon grew to weeks and weeks into months. This was made possible by the size and the resources available to them at Kensington Manor, and any burden caused by this unnecessary individuality was felt only by the staff.

## Resignations

As a result of this burden, it wasn't long until both Mr. and Mrs. Kensington began to lose vital employees. Numerous members of Kensington Manor's paid staff issued ultimatums or resigned altogether. This mass resignation can be marked as the removal of the keystone and started the toppling of Kensington Manor.

As the paid staff at Kensington Manor continued to shrink, so too, did the profits. The once bountiful harvest was soon nonexistent. Crops never planted are crops never harvested, and the net effect of this was soon felt at the highest levels of the manor house, where the lack of funds became the newest obsession.

It was at this time that Mrs. Kensington's personal physician and personal advisor suggested to her that liquidation of the estate might be her only salvation.

He also suggested she make this strategy known to Mr. Kensington, and she should do so in court, thus protecting her assets via divorce proceedings.

## Rathers

Mrs. Kensington feared such a move and made this known to Dr. Poirot. She felt her husband would rather die than part with his manor home, regardless of its condition.

Concurrently, certain individuals from Mr. Kensington's past began visiting the estate, some announced, and others not. News of the estate's prior revitalization had traveled far and wide, but the news of its most recent downward turn had not.

Desperate for money, Mr. Kensington organized an auction on the grounds of Kensington Manor, hoping to raise enough capital to resurrect his treasured manor home. On the auction block that day were many furnishings and works of art, along with various tools, farm equipment, livestock, and his beloved Palomino.

Attendees came from as far north as New York City, and from as far west as St. Louis, most bargain hunters, but some just curious. Cajun Jack organized, tracked, and recorded the auction items into the ledger on Mr. Kensington's behalf. All bidders were required to give their name and address and further required to deposit one hundred dollars into escrow, as proof of intent, before being issued a bidder's number. This policy was not problematic for those there to buy, but it was problematic for some attendees. Several buyers asked to speak to Mr. Kensington after they were informed of the escrow requirement, and he was summoned to the auctioneer's stand on their behalf. Mr. Kensington waived the deposit for at least three of the bidders that day.

About mid-auction, just after the last head of livestock had been sold, the next item up for sale turned out to be a different type of head altogether. Through some misunderstanding, Mr. Kensington's mounted rhino was the next lot offered. He ended up buying his own property; simple withdrawal was not allowed, due to certain legalities. After winning, he promptly returned the head to the wall inside Kensington Manor, mumbling to himself as he rehung the mount, *"If I don't kill the Rhino, somebody else will."*

From high atop the balcony, Mrs. Kensington and Dr. Poirot took turns viewing the auction through her brass opera glasses.

"Do you recognize that fellow?" Dr. Poirot asked Mrs. Kensington as he handed over the glasses.

"Which one of them?" she replied.

"The gentleman in the black duster," Dr. Poirot replied before continuing, "isn't it somewhat warm for such attire?"

Mrs. Kensington did not know the man, and made the doctor aware of the fact, as she continued to watch the proceedings.

"Has Mr. Kensington disclosed to you his intentions for the proceeds?" Dr. Poirot inquired.

Mrs. Kensington did not reply, as her attention was focused upon the ongoing auction, where they could faintly hear the auctioneer's chant.

"That's a lively and unusual dialect, wouldn't you agree, doctor?"

"Mrs. Kensington…" Dr. Poirot said as he took Mrs. Kensington by the arm, forcing her to lower the spectacles.

"Yes?" Mrs. Kensington said as she now acknowledged the doctor.

"The proceeds?"

Mr. Kensington had disclosed to no one his intentions for the money accumulated in response to the sale, not even Jack. He took several precautions to see that the final tally remained confidential. At numerous times during the sale, Mr. Kensington removed the tallies from the ledger and emptied the cash box, leaving only Jack's memory untouched.

That evening, after almost all of the assets had been liquidated, and all of the bidders had departed, Mr. Kensington retreated to the confines of his humidor to stash his earnings. He preferred the security of the safe behind the portrait but had been unable to gain access to it since losing its combination. In the humidor, Mr. Kensington removed the covering of just one of the many barrels inside and placed the money underneath several pounds of shredded tobacco. He then resealed the barrel and rolled it back into position, to further secure its disguise. Next, he reached high atop the shelf that spanned the west wall, where he retrieved a nearly full bottle of whiskey. Sitting on the money barrel, he began to drink. He'd been drinking within the confines of his humidor for years now, hiding this vice from his wife to avoid upsetting her, but now it was just a habit.

The next morning, Mr. Kensington strolled the sparse grounds of his estate, debating his future and his next move, when an abrupt disturbance arose within the chicken coop nearby. A fox ran swiftly around the corner and moved quickly up and down the perimeter of the fenced area, seeking a weakness within the chicken wire to exploit.

Under normal circumstances, Mr. Kensington would have dealt with this predator with a single shot from his revolver, but since the gun had been sold just the day before, Mr. Kensington resorted to a more archaic defense. As he walked toward the disturbance, he simultaneously stooped and retrieved several stones from the ground, placing them in his coat pocket. Once he'd improved his vantage point and the fox was within sight, Mr. Kensington hurled the largest of the four stones at the fox with all his might, missing the predator completely, but dropping a large rooster dead in his tracks. The fox fled the scene without a meal that morning.

Upset with himself for missing the fox, but killing the rooster, Mr. Kensington entered the coop himself to retrieve the dead chicken. After removing the bird and fastening the door behind him on his way out, Mr. Kensington walked briskly toward the manor house, taking no notice of the chicken hawk that bore down upon him. The hawk's first pass failed, but startled Mr. Kensington and knocked the hat from his head and the chicken from his hand. Coincidentally, the chicken landed just on top of the hat, now exposed there in the open for the hawk to take. The second pass from the hawk proved successful, and Mr. Kensington witnessed the bird of prey retrieve the chicken, now entangled with the hat, and fly away north and out of sight.

Mr. Kensington was not seen again until his body was discovered in the basement of Kensington Manor.

## **The Remains**

After the initial discovery of the body, the event was made known to local authorities and Kensington Manor was overrun with numerous English-speaking investigators, two French-speaking gendarmes, also fluent in Portuguese, one local Spaniard, and one Dutchman, possibly necessary, to cover all variants in languages.

When the few remaining residents and workers at Kensington Manor were interviewed regarding their last interaction with Mr. Kensington and the whereabouts of the money, this is what they had to say:

## **Mrs. Kensington (Lady of the House - English/Baptist)**

"The last time I saw Thorogood was through those brass spectacles given to me by Dr. Poirot. From the second-floor balcony, I witnessed his interactions with Jack as they sold off our belongings, one after another. He did not inform me of his intentions regarding the proceeds, and I never saw a nickel from the sale. I suggest you ask Jack about the money. I also saw Alphonso leave the estate with Jack, just after the auction. I've been told that Mr. Kensington had secured continued employment for the young man since his groom services would no longer be needed after the horse was sold. My understanding is that this employment was just past Shreveport, about four hundred miles from here."

### Dr. Condos Poirot (Liaison to the Lady of the House - English/Baptist)

"As you already know, I spent the entire day of the auction in the company of my employer, Mrs. Kensington. She has been experiencing difficult times, considering her health and the circumstances of her marriage. I rarely spoke to Mr. Kensington and relayed any messages addressed to him via his liaison, Cajun Jack. This turn of events has taken its toll on my lady."

### Cajun Jack (Liaison to the Man of the House - Creole/Santeria)

"I've worked with Mr. Kensington for many years. He was good to me spiritually, he was good to me financially, and he was good to me all around. I don't know how this happened. I last saw him the night after the auction. I don't know what happened to him. I was in Shreveport when this tragedy occurred."

### Adolfo Carie (Farmhand to Kensington Manor - French/ Voodooist)

"I didn't take that chicken. I saw Mr. Kensington take that bird. He was already dead. The bird, not Mr. Kensington. I think a fox killed him. Not Mr. Kensington, the bird. I didn't have anything to do with it. People all over are scared of me now. But I tell you, I didn't do it."

"Je n'ai pas pris ce poulet. J'ai vu M. Kensington prendre cet oiseau. Il était déjà mort. L'oiseau pas M. Kensington. Je pense qu'un renard l'a tué. Pas M. Kensington, l'oiseau. Je n'ai rien à voir avec ça. Les gens partout ont peur de moi maintenant. Mais, je vous le dis, je ne l'ai pas fait."

## Gweneth Archer (Lady-in-Waiting - English/Methodist)

"I have great respect for Mrs. Kensington, and based upon that respect, I have strictly abided by her wishes that I have absolutely no interaction with Mr. Kensington. I don't recall speaking to him, not even once. I regret hearing of his passing. It is unfortunate, and I can only offer my lady prayers that she will take his death in stride."

## Monks Sterning (Footman to the Lady of the House - French/Baptist)

Mr. Sterning had been on vacation and was not present on the day of the auction, or on the day Mr. Kensington died. The French-speaking footman in service to Mrs. Kensington provided a statement to his employer on the day of his return.

His statement is shown below along with the English translation, provided by Mrs. Kensington.

*"Conformément aux souhaits de ma femme, je n'ai jamais interagi avec son mari ni professionnellement ni socialement. J'ai quitté Kensington Manor trois jours avant la vente aux enchères et j'ai passé cette semaine à Baton Rouge avec ma sœur et sa famille. Je viens tout juste de retourner au travail et je n'ai pas parlé ni interagi avec M. Kensington depuis mon embauche."*

*"In accordance with my lady's wishes, I never interacted with her husband, either professionally or socially. I departed Kensington Manor*

*three days before the auction and spent that week in Baton Rouge with my sister and her family. I am just now returning to work, and have not spoken to or interacted with Mr. Kensington since my hiring."*

## Alphonso Morie (Groom and Farmhand to Kensington Manor - French/Voodooist)

*"J'ai parlé et interagi avec M. Kensington toute la journée de la vente aux enchères. Il a émis de nombreux ordres ce jour-là, la plupart concernant son cheval. Il m'a fait toiletter l'animal une fois juste avant de faire sa dernière balade. Le trajet a été court. Il ramena l'animal en une dizaine de minutes et s'assit sur le coursier pendant les enchères. Après la vente, il m'a fait toiletter l'animal une dernière fois pour le nouveau propriétaire. J'étais bouleversé de voir le cheval vendu. Je m'attendais à ce que le chômage suive, mais sinon, M. Kensington a été bon avec moi."*

*I spoke to and interacted with Mr. Kensington all day of the auction. He issued many orders that day, most of them about his horse. He had me groom the animal once, just before taking his last ride. The ride was short. He brought the animal back in about ten minutes and sat upon the steed during the bidding. After the sale, he groomed the animal himself for the new owner. I was upset to see the horse sold. I feared unemployment might follow, but Mr. Kensington was kind enough to arrange for a new job for me.*

## Able Forester (Farmhand and Logger - English/Methodist)

"Neither I nor my assistant attended the auction that day. We were surveying the first section of acreage that Mr. Kensington wanted to be cleared, and busy preparing an estimate of the lumber's value for him. We prefer a more rustic environment and declined his offer to shelter in his manor home. Camping in the forest saves us time.

When we wake up, we are already at the work site, which eliminates the need for commuting. I only heard of his passing today."

## Mr. Collinsword (Farmhand and Logger's Assistant - English/Atheist)

"I was within the apprenticeship of my employer, Mr. Forester, during this time. I never met with Mr. Kensington on my own. If you doubt my statement, you may verify with him."

## Rigor Mortis

The body was found by Pearson Brooks, assistant blacksmith of Kensington Manor. The body was within the manor house, on the lower basement level, just inside the closed door of the walk-in humidor.

Dr. Poirot, already on the scene at Kensington Manor and acting as coroner, was summoned to the humidor, where he ruled the death 'natural causes,' due to heart attack.

There were also no signs of injury or trauma on the body. However, there were some oddities reported at the scene. Feathers of two different types were found on Mr. Kensington's cloak and trousers. His favorite hat—in fact, his only hat—was not present. Robbery of his person was excluded as a motive, due to the contents of his pockets. When inventoried they included: cigars, matches, one small bottle of whiskey, nearly full, coins and bills totaling twenty-three dollars and eighty-eight cents, and three small, smooth river stones. However, robbery of Kensington assets may have been a factor, considering the inability of manor staff to account for some furnishings and works of art. In light of Mr. Kensington's checkered past, revenge and/or retaliation may have played a factor, as well.

ACT 13

# THE PAISLEY WITCHES

Mr. Kensington hadn't been sick before his death, and the investigation had stalled without formulation of any suspect, so the rumor mongerers and gossipers took it upon themselves to become self-proclaimed experts on the matter. An endless wave of speculation rippled through Orleans Parish and all adjacent parishes.

The particular ripple with the highest crest in this series of recurring waves was the one rooted in Voodoo and Black magic.

## <u>The Powder Keg</u>

It's no secret that New Orleans has a long and colorful history in cultural religions that runs deep. The depth of this can be measured by examining many of the long-held traditions and rituals still being practiced today. It was these very rituals that, in effect, ignited the fuse on the powder keg which would explode into rampant speculation regarding the circumstances surrounding Mr. Kensington's death, transforming it into 'Kensington's Mystery.'

## The Preposterous

Mr. Kensington was a particularly religious man who favored his Baptist religion over others and had very little tolerance for any other denomination, despite numerous similarities. On the grounds of Kensington Manor, no less than five religions were being practiced at any given time. Magic was the common element in each of these ideologies. And because they were similar and had many commonalities, the intolerance from one to another was unexplainable and indicative of hypocrisy.

## Baptist

The majority of the faithful residing on the grounds of Kensington Manor were Baptists—just over half of all the servants and one-hundred percent of the Kensingtons. Mr. and Mrs. Kensington had both been raised by Baptist parents, and as a result, their personal adoption of this religion was unspoken, unquestioned, and absolute. Both Kensingtons were staunch supporters of the Baptist religion, classifying all others as fraudulent, without properly educating themselves on anything that varied from what they'd been taught. This narrow-mindedness could, possibly, account for some of the misunderstandings that occurred after Mr. Kensington's death.

## Methodist

The Methodists accounted for about twenty percent of the staff employed at Kensington manner. Despite the many similarities shared between the Baptists and the Methodists, there remained a dividing line separating the two from true brother and sisterhood.

## Catholicism

The Catholic faith at Kensington manor was professed by approximately ten percent of all workers, with most of them unable to conquer that line of division separating them from the others.

## Santeria

The Santerias, while closely aligned with the Catholics, accounted for less than ten percent of all worshipers at Kensington Manor.

## Voodoo

Of the five predominant religious affiliations at Kensington Manor, it was those engaging in Voodoo that attracted the most attention regarding Mr. Kensington's demise.

Active practice of Voodoo, with its rituals and sacrifices, was strictly prohibited on Manor grounds, and anyone caught violating this policy was dealt with in rather barbaric terms. Therefore, those Voodooists who remained true to their religion were forced into secrecy when they worshiped. Any rituals, especially those with elements of fire or chanting, were carried out during the blackness of night, in some secluded area away from the estate, usually down by the river's edge so that secrecy could be maintained and religious persecution could be avoided.

Suspicion of the Voodooists grew based upon the secrecy, the sacrifices, and the rituals. There was never any consideration that the basis upon which the persecuting religions were founded also contained many of the same elements.

The King James Version of the Holy Bible, the chosen scripture of the Baptists at Kensington Manor, mentions and supports the element of secrecy when in prayer. The passage from the Book of **Matthew 6:6** reads:

"But thou, when thou prayest, enter into thy
closet, and when thou hast shut thy door, pray to
thy Father which is in secret; and thy Father which
seeth in secret shall reward thee openly."

Prayer at night is also approved and encouraged, as shown in this passage from the Book of **Psalms 119:62**:

"At midnight I will rise to give thanks unto thee
because of thy righteous judgments."

Rituals are also documented within the Bible, like the one in the Book of **Psalms 23:5**:

"Thou preparest a table before me in the presence
of mine enemies: thou anointest my head with oil;
my cup runneth over."

Sacrifice, too, is mentioned, like in **Leviticus 23:19**:

"Then ye shall sacrifice one kid of the goats for a
sin offering, and two lambs of the first year for a
sacrifice of peace offerings."

And magic? Well, that was the most predominate of the discriminating factors of this religious persecution, even though this phenomenon is mentioned many times throughout biblical scripture, both in a positive light, like when Moses divides the Red Sea and when Jesus changes the water to wine, and in a negative light, as shown below from **Deutoronmy 18:9-12**:

9 "When thou art come into the land which the Lord
thy God giveth thee, thou shalt not learn to do

after the abominations of those nations.
10 There shall not be found among you any one that maketh his son or his daughter to pass through the fire, or that useth divination, or an observer of times, or an enchanter, or a witch.
11 Or a charmer, or a consulter with familiar spirits, or a wizard, or a necromancer.
12 For all that do these things are an abomination unto the Lord: and because of these abominations the Lord thy God doth drive them out from before thee."

In consideration of all this, the Voodooists and their religion were labeled Black Magic.

The term Black Magic would evolve over time to take on a sinister connotation, encompassing all of the negative facets of Voodoo, including the secrecy, the blackness of night, the outdated rituals, and the barbaric sacrifices, culminating in something so misunderstood that it could only be identified as evil by those other denominations. As is so often the case, humans judge others for their differences. And when it comes to religion, people are particularly unforgiving of those who choose to worship in ways that do not align with their own practices, even when the very rituals they criticize closely resemble the ones buried in their own history.

And even though the Kensingtons and their forefathers were self-proclaimed Christians and openly supported the scriptures and text of the Holy Bible, where many instances of secrecy, sacrifice, and magic had been recorded and praised, they spearheaded this unforgiving attitude. The recently widowed Mrs. Kensington, her servants and staff, and those investigating Mr. Kensington's death could not open their eyes and their minds wide enough to put aside their intolerance. Ultimately the Voodooist was blamed for Mr. Kensington's death, especially when they learned of Agnes Naismith.

### The Paisley Witches

It was in the year 1696 when the slightest eccentricity or oddity could cost you your life, that Agnes Naismith of Paisley, Scotland, and six other individuals, were accused of practicing witchcraft, otherwise known as Black Magic, by the daughter of a local prominent lord. The charge? Bewitching. Supposedly, they had, in some way, coerced a servant to steal milk from the lord whom she served.

These seven people quickly became known as The Paisley Witches.

Just after her trial, but before her hanging, Agnes Naismith cursed everyone present at the proceedings, including their descendants. In attendance that day were ancestors of Mr. Thorogood Kensington.

### The Prometheus

After her hanging, and the hangings of her alleged accomplices and supposed fellow witches, the bodies were burned to further eradicate any evil within them that might linger on after death. This precaution, thought necessary at the time, was to protect witnesses from evil. It did not, however, remove Agnes Naismith's curse on later descendants.

This notion that the curse from Agnes Naismith might still be in effect, combined with the intolerance felt toward the Voodooists, caused members of the household to assume this was where the guilt lay. As the most vocal and authoritative voices, these people effectively redirected the police in the initial stages of the investigation into Mr. Kensington's death.

### The Problem

Coincidentally, on the eve of Mr. Kensington's death, there was a congregation assembled in secrecy down by the riverside, where the ritual performed that night involved the sacrifice of a rooster. Earlier that morning, a prowling fox had been reported near the chicken coop on manor grounds. Subsequently, Adolfo Carie, the farm hand responsible for the chickens, reported the lost fowl to the proper authority within the Kensington household. It was particularly noted that this farmhand's religion was Voodoo.

From these coincidences, misunderstandings, and intolerances, a certain opinion was formed. Mr. Kensington had been murdered and his murderer must be a Voodooist.

The condition of Mr. Kensington's body, complete with feathers upon his clothing that had no explanation, led to a jumping-to-conclusions, if you will, and most pointed the finger of guilt at the young Voodooist, Adolfo Carie.

## **The Paternity**

There was also the Madame Blanque affair to consider, and suspicions regarding the paternity of her daughter, Marie Louise Jeanne Blanque.

For years, throughout New Orleans, a scandal of enormous proportions hung over all of those who bore the Kensington name. It was rumored that, at some time during Thorogood's childhood, his father had shared a burning romance with fellow New Orleans resident and socialite, Marie Delphine LaLaurie.

LaLaurie, who resided at 1140 Royal Street in the French Quarter, only three miles from the Garden District, was often seen near the elder Kensington's home, just out of town. Similarly, the elder Mr. Kensington was seen, many times, strolling along Royal Street.

In some instances, discretion was used to maintain the secrecy of the affair, while at other times, they walked hand-in-hand through the Quarter, apparently, without care. This, flaunting of their relationship, and their disrespect and disregard for LaLaurie's husband and Kensington's wife, became the talk of the town, leading to questions regarding the paternity of LaLaurie's youngest daughter. Some suggested that Mr. Kensington was her biological father, making her Thorogood Kensington's half-sister.

Their romance, and the associated publicity, mostly by word of mouth, ultimately caused LaLaurie's marriage to end. The former Marie Delphine Blanque, or simply, Madame Blanque, divorced her third husband, physician Leonard Louis Nicolas LaLaurie, now making herself available, once more, for matrimony, and anticipating the new surname of Kensington.

This availability had a rather reversing effect on the elder Kensington, and he soon ended their relationship.

Afterward, LaLaurie, now unmarried and alone, remained at her Royal Street address, where she resided with her daughters and servants. In the following years, after the gossip related to this scandal had faded, LaLaurie, now going by her preferred name, Madame Blanque, was, once again, in the news.

She was accused of abusing her servants on multiple occasions, with some of the abuses resulting in death. Once the news of her horrific abuses became widely known, her home on Royal Street was burned to the ground by vigilantes.

Madame Blanque fled to France to escape justice for her crimes.

As for paternity… It was neither proven nor disproven, but after Thorogood reached adulthood and learned he might have a sister, he began to visit Marie Louise Jeanne Blanque. He never disclosed those visitations to anyone to avoid stirring up old rumors. He accomplished this by *sailing straight to her front door, on the memory of the Onomatopoeia,* so to speak.

# ACT 14

# PANDORA'S SUGGESTION

After Mrs. Kensington's health fell further into decline, and after Dr. Poirot's nurse had moved in, Dr. Poirot decided to cohabitate with us, as well, by moving into the manor house so he could 'better service' his client.

Coincidentally, it was at this approximate time that Mrs. Kensington entered into a prolonged state of lucidity, insinuating that she was on the mend. Furthermore, after a curious incident occurred, I took notice of the sustained clarity exhibited by my hostess. The correlation between her improved state of mind and this happenstance captured my attention as more than incidental, causing me to embark on the following experiment.

**Parlor**

Days after showing up with various hat boxes and garment bags, Dr. Poirot suggested that he and Mrs. Kensington should transfer the location of their evening tea from the downstairs parlor to the balcony that overlooks the entrance to Kensington Manor. This suggestion was approved wholeheartedly by Mrs. Kensington, and thereby set in motion a series of events that piqued my curiosity.

Each evening, as they sat on the balcony just before retiring, Dr. Poirot would ring his nurse, ordering tea service for two from her.

## Patio

Twenty minutes afterward, the nurse would deliver the two cups of tea, sugar cubes, and teaspoons, all upon a portable, sterling silver, lazy Susan tea server, and place it upon the small, round patio table which sat between Mrs. Kensington and her Doctor.

What happened next was accidental, at first. I'd assumed, and rightfully so, that I'd never been favored all that much by Dr. Poirot. Not once, had he called me by name, and never had he one good word to speak in my direction. This accident changed all of that. Well, to be more accurate, it changed in that he called me by name, but he didn't have anything positive to say.

I, too, sat on the balcony that day, trying not to interfere with the two of them, when suddenly, I felt the need to retire to my room. As I stood and began to walk slowly away, I bumped the patio table holding the tea for two. This slight bump jarred the table, disturbing the lazy Susan. Dr. Poirot, fearing the tea would be spilled, jumped from his chair and yelled at me, invoking my full name in the process. As he faced me, with his back to the table and the tea, I witnessed the lazy Susan revolving slowly around by one-hundred and eighty degrees. This shift in orientation ultimately placed the tea intended for Dr. Poirot in front of Mrs. Kensington, and the tea intended for Mrs. Kensington in front of Dr. Poirot. Being a gentleman, and not wanting to upset my hostess further, I retreated to the solace of my room without responding to the angry doctor.

## Present

The next morning, I happened to notice that Dr. Poirot was not present for breakfast. I didn't think much of his absence. After all, he was somewhat new to the household, so it caused me no alarm. By that afternoon, I felt otherwise. I overheard the doctor's frantic nurse report to Mrs. Kensington that Dr. Poirot did not remember her, and he remained in bed, where he talked nonsense. I paused to reflect. These were the same symptoms previously exhibited by my lady, but on this day, her lucidity couldn't be better. She was sharp as a tack, as they say.

I called a boarders' meeting without delay. Naturally, Dr. Poirot and his nurse were not invited.

## Pandora

The meeting was called to order, and I acted swiftly to inform my housemates of my suspicions about Dr. Poirot. The quorum of eight was more than enough to act on this issue, but I'd hoped Pandora would be present. Often, she seemed to have an insight that none of the others had, including me. Minutes later, after we'd all engaged heavily in debating this topic, Pandora entered the room 'fashionably late,' she liked to call it.

She took her seat without a word and silently listened to the ongoing debate. I thought her disinterest originated from some unknown preoccupation she might have, but what seemed like disinterest to me was, rather, a deep interest to her.

## Private

The vote was seven in favor of the second motion, with one against and one abstaining. All eight abstained on the first motion. Pandora withheld both of her votes and her opinions on the matters until the others had gone, leaving just the two of us to discuss her suggestion in private.

The second motion, approved by the others, and put forth by Mr. O'Keefe, suggested that we should seek alternate shelter.

I disagreed. I genuinely felt that Mrs. Kensington required our assistance, and I didn't want to abandon her when she'd been so good to us.

## **<u>Prove</u>**

Pandora made me aware of a tactic that we could employ to determine if my suspicions were true. This tactic would either prove this theory or fail to prove this theory. If failure were the outcome, no one would be the wiser, and there would be no harm done.

Therefore, we moved forward and enacted her idea.

The next evening, just at tea time, I exited onto the balcony through the partially opened French doors, just as Dr. Poirot's nurse delivered the tea.

"Oh, it's you, Mr. Peabody," Dr. Poirot said.

"You aren't still angry with him, are you, Doctor?" Mrs. Kensington asked. She looked at me. "I'm sure yesterday's mishap was just an accident, wasn't it, Mr. Peabody?"

"Well, Mr. Peabody?" Dr. Poirot reiterated.

I didn't respond to him at all. I dislike engaging in small talk, especially with those with small minds. So, I just let Mrs. Kensington's words speak on my behalf.

"Please have a seat, Mr. Peabody," Mrs. Kensington said.

This was my chance—the opportunity that Pandora and I had discussed just the day before. *It's now or never,* I thought to myself. And with that thought, I made my move. I bumped the patio table; this time it was intentional. This bump toppled the entire tea service and earned me another scolding from Dr. Poirot. Once again, I retreated to my room and waited for the result, while Pandora watched to see if they replenished the tea.

The next day, both Dr. Poirot and Mrs. Kensington remained lucid, with their cognitive abilities fully intact.

The next evening, Pandora suggested a different approach.

We both waited in the kitchen for the evening call for tea and watched as it was prepared. Just as we'd suspected, the nurse placed an unknown ingredient in one cup, but not the second. At Pandora's cue, while she distracted the nurse, I rotated the lazy Susan one-hundred and eighty degrees. And just as we'd theorized, Dr. Poirot lay bed-ridden and disoriented the following day.

One day later, at tea time, I approached the French doors and was met straight away by Dr. Poirot. In no uncertain terms, he invited me to go away, and not to return, or otherwise disturb his tea time with Mrs. Kensington. By this time, Pandora and I had not thought of an alternate plan, but as you may expect, the next morning, Mrs. Kensington is the one who did not appear at breakfast and remained in bed throughout the day.

In consultation with Pandora, I suggested we reveal our experiment to the others and enlist their participation to assist us in the continued disruption of evening tea time at Kensington Manor. She felt otherwise, citing bias as her reasoning. I then suggested she place the idea into the suggestion box for the sake of anonymity. That's when she informed me of her illiteracy. I didn't know how to respond to that.

By now, my suspicion of Dr. Poirot had been elevated to an all-time high. I was certain he was responsible for Mr. Kensington's death, and now he was intent on killing Mrs. Kensington, as well. This was my theory, but there was still no hard evidence to support my suspicions.

Weeks elapsed, with me upsetting the tea service and spilling it nightly, in an effort to protect my hostess, until the day came that I was forcibly removed from the balcony by Dr. Poirot, and no longer invited there by Mrs. Kensington. She let me down easily, with an apologetic but firm tone.

## Poison

I was devastated and feared the worst. It was, most likely, only a matter of time before the contrived poisoning of Mrs. Kensington would end her life.

That's when Pandora and I took to altering the tea cup positions by rotating the lazy Susan before it left the kitchen with the nurse. After several more days of failure to rotate the cups, and after Mrs. Kensington seemed on the decline again, something else happened.

## Portion

As Pandora and I watched the nurse make the tea, we noticed her place a rather large portion of the yet unknown ingredient into one of the cups. Our only hope was to employ the cup rotation, hoping to succeed and prevent Mrs. Kensington from drinking from the cup. Like clockwork, the bell in the kitchen rang, alerting the nurse to deliver the tea. That's when Pandora distracted the nurse by purposely tumbling a crystal goblet from a nearby shelf. I acted immediately by rotating the lazy Susan one-hundred and eighty degrees. Then, we retreated and waited.

Time seems to move slower when you're anticipating some unknown result or happening, and that's exactly how I remember this evening. We waited for what seemed like a long time before learning the result of our plan. The kitchen bell rang for the second time that evening, which was out of the norm. In reality, only minutes had elapsed before a frantic Mrs. Kensington could be heard on the line pleading with the nurse for assistance.

## Poirot's Death

Dr. Condos Poirot drank the concoction meant for Mrs. Kensington. Just after swallowing the tea, upon realizing his mistake, the doctor leaped from his chair, stumbled awkwardly, and fell from the top floor balcony to his death below.

Mrs. Kensington had no further bouts of delirium—none induced by tea, that is.

## Period

After Dr. Poirot's death, Mrs. Kensington retreated to the seclusion of her room where I overheard her in nightly consultation with her husband. During this period of mourning, she refrained from interacting with us and did not receive visitors. This was a sad and lonely time at Kensington Manor, and I feared the worst, while I strived for a positive resolution. I had envisioned all of us being evicted, becoming hungry and homeless, roaming the streets of New Orleans—unhappy, unhealthy, and scared—if Mrs. Kensington continued to insist on our eviction. However, I believed we could remain within the house, living peacefully, as we had in the past if we all united in solidarity.

## Pessimism

Pessimism is contagious amongst those individuals who maintain close relationships, like housemates.

## Proximity

Sadly, it's all too easy to find someone with a negative aura. Spend any time in close proximity to these individuals and you may catch this contagion.

## Parasite

The parasitic nature of this communicable disease can be devastating and should be avoided at all costs.

## Prevention

Prevention is the best cure.

At some point, I discovered one of my housemates was stricken with this disease. I only wish I'd realized this before contracting pessimism, myself.

## Pessimist

I'm usually an upbeat sort of guy. If there's a problem, I search for a solution. If there's an equation, I attempt to solve for the unknown. Wherever there's a pessimist, I avoid their presence. In hindsight, this is how I should have handled him, but I chose to confront his continually negative motions and his continued support of others' negative motions, to ill effect.

## Percy O'Keefe

At all subsequent tenant meetings after the death of Dr. Poirot, Percy, otherwise known as Mr. O'Keefe, continued to enter pessimistic motions and motions that were not in the best interest of the housemates. These motions became increasingly ridiculous and arbitrary and made it difficult to determine Mr. O'Keefe's motives for making such motions. After dealing with these preposterous ideas on more than one occasion, I determined, or rather, Pandora determined that Percy's motives were buried within his own hidden agenda.

As we became an unofficial investigative team, our ability to cover more ground and collect more evidence doubled. During an afternoon of prowling about in search of evidence to support our investigation into the original crime, Pandora witnessed something we decided was important.

As she walked briskly home one evening at dusk and approached Kensington Manor, she viewed a group of three individuals on the corner of Cheshire and Camp, where they engaged one another in a lengthy communication.

From his behavior and his body language, it was determined that Mr. O'Keefe had extended offers of residency to these two individuals who were unrecognized by Pandora, although there was no vacancy.

After this encounter, Pandora and I concluded Mr. O'Keefe's motive was to create one or more vacancies at Kensington Manor, and his divisive motions were in support of that motive. I decided to confront Mr. Percy O'Keefe at the next tenant meeting.

## Position

At the next tenant meeting, just after I brought the attendees to order, but before I had a chance to confront Percy on his divisiveness, he stood from his seated position, and promptly entered the first and only motion of business for this particular meeting. His motion was in support of electing a new chair for tenant meetings. I was flabbergasted at his bold attempt to remove me and waited briefly for anyone who might second his motion.

After waiting long enough, in my opinion, I made Mr. O'Keefe aware that my position was not by election but by appointment. I was acting on approval, and on behalf of the direct wishes of the lady of the house. Furthermore, had the motion been seconded, and had a vote been taken, there would not have been enough votes in favor of its passing. According to my count, the vote would have been four in favor, four against, with one abstaining. The four in favor would have been Mr. and Mrs. O'Keefe, Beauregard, and Ginger. The four against were Josephine, Kitty, Rose, and myself, and, well… You know the rest. After I presented the non-existent voting data to Mr. O'Keefe, as I saw it, he pushed even further, by suggesting a simple consultation with Mrs. Kensington would result in my replacement. That's when the infighting amongst us tenants began, and I hate to say this, but a 'cat-fight' ensued.

## Pugilists

It wasn't enough that this guy was in the midst of a coup and sought my immediate removal; it was his entire attitude. Eventually, insults were exchanged, feelings were hurt, and then, just before all control was lost, someone insulted Mr. O'Keefe's partner by suggesting there had been a lapse in fidelity on her part. Mr. O'Keefe responded by taking a swing at me, hitting Rose instead, which I could not ignore.

## Pandemonium

It resulted in a room-clearing melee, with pandemonium ensuing afterward. We didn't see the opposing tenants again, until a surprise gala organized by Mrs. Kensington.

## Passing

You can imagine how this turn of events affected my investigation. By this time, I was certain that Dr. Poirot had murdered Mr. Kensington, but had no proof. The case was now cold. After all, it had been many years since his passing, and there had been only one arrest. The prime suspect, the Voodooist who'd initially been charged in the matter, had not been convicted, even after being tried just weeks after his arrest.

ACT 15

# THE ACCUSED, THE ALIBIED, AND THE EXONERATED

The headline in the Times-Picayune read, 'Adolfo Carie Victorious.' I hadn't located this crucial detail until examining, for a third time, the desk in the late Mr. Kensington's study. The old newspaper had fallen behind a drawer, where it became wedged and had gone unseen for, what I assume, was a great long while. It would have been beneficial to have known of this exoneration early on in my investigation, but in this instance, delayed details are better than no details at all. The young Voodooist who had drawn such attention in the days and weeks following Mr. Kensington's death, was no longer a suspect, and even though he'd been acquitted in a court of law, there seemed to be lingering doubts about his involvement, and rumors about his guilt that still transcended the not guilty verdict.

After learning of the trial and the acquittal, I thought a review of my investigation, detailing the accused, the alibied, and the exoner-ated, was in order. The statements below were compiled from case-work documentation located in the study at Kensington Manor.

## The Exonerated

**Adolfo Carie**, the young Voodooist, had been acquitted. It would be unjust to leave his innocence with no further comment. Based on what I'd learned, he became a suspect for one reason, and one reason only, and that reason was religious bias and persecution.

The conclusion that Adolfo was targeted for religious persecution was supported by the following entry that I'd located in Mr. Kensington's journal.

This entry was dated five days after Mr. Kensington's death. The entry did not have a signature, but handwriting analysis suggested it'd been written by Jack.

In summary of Jack's lengthy entry, let me paraphrase;

On the day before Mr. Kensington's death, as he strolled the sparse grounds of his estate, several children of Voodooist lineage engaged in a game of hopscotch in the loose dirt near the chicken coop. Their game was interrupted by Mr. Kensington as he stooped and removed their stones from the gaming area drawn on the ground. Several of the children gave the same eyewitness account when they described Mr. Kensington's behavior and actions that day. The children stated that Mr. Kensington hurled one of the stones toward the chicken coop killing a rooster just inside the cage. Mr. Kensington became enraged and yelled for assistance as he called out the name 'Adolfo'. According to the children, no one ever came to assist Mr. Kensington. By this time the children were terrified so they retreated to the nearby orchard where they hid behind the trees and watched. They witnessed Mr. Kensington being attacked by a chicken hawk as he attempted to return to the manor house holding the dead rooster. Next, they saw the hawk flying away carrying both the rooster and Mr. Kensington's hat.

This eyewitness account proves Adolfo's innocence regarding the rooster.

According to the last handwritten sentence within this journal entry, Jack suspected this eyewitness statement was ignored by the authorities considering its source.

Therefore, due to his acquittal and the eyewitness statement corroborated by all the children present that day, Adolfo was removed from my list of suspects.

## <u>The Alibied</u>

**Mrs. Kensington,** lady of the house and wife of the deceased, was a suspect from the very start. Basic murder investigation theory dictates that fact, and therefore, the investigation into her was thorough. Mrs. Kensington's motive was clear from the very start. The couple had separated and were possibly headed for divorce. Financial gain or prevention of financial loss were determined to be Mrs. Kensington's primary motives. However, her alibi was strong and corroborated by her personal physician, Dr. Condos Poirot, a prominent member of the community. This alibi waned in strength after the death of Dr. Poirot and the discovery of his intent to harm and possibly murder his client, Mrs. Kensington. The likelihood of his involvement in Mr. Kensington's death is high, but if true, cannot be prosecuted due to the Doctor's untimely death.

**Dr. Condos Poirot,** due to his passing, is no longer a prosecutable suspect in Mr. Kensington's murder.

**Gweneth Archer, Mrs. Kensington's lady-in-waiting** and youngest employee of Kensington Manor was alibied by her employer, Mrs. Kensington, and never formally introduced to the man of the house. She had no motive for this crime, and is, therefore, not a suspect.

**Alphonso Morie, farmhand to Kensington Manor and groom for Mr. Kensington's prizm Palomino,** was unknowingly alibied by Mrs. Kensington through her statements given to police at the time of Mr. Kensington's death. Mr. Morie's presence in Shreveport was subsequently verified.

**Pearson Brooks, assistant blacksmith,** found Mr. Kensington's body on the lower level of his manor home. The coroner, Dr. Poirot, determined Mr. Kensington was found within twelve hours of his death. Mr. Brooks was alibied by multiple manor house staff, and is, therefore, not a suspect.

**Monks Sterning, footman to Mrs. Kensington** and newest employee at Kensington Manor, had no motive to commit this crime. Although police did not speak to the young man in person, his statement was handwritten, and subsequently delivered to the manor house, where Mrs. Kensington translated his native French into English. Mr. Sterning is not a suspect at this point in the investigation.

**Mr. Bainbridge, weekly courier to Kensington Manor,** was informed by Mrs. Kensington's physician that his services were no longer needed. He stopped delivery to Kensington Manor long before Mr. Kensington's death, and only returned there on two occasions, to extend his condolences and to inventory the manor house to determine what goods were needed. Mr. Bainbridge had no motive, and is, therefore, not a suspect. After his brief visits with Mrs. Kensington, he described her behavior as odd and out-of-the-ordinary.

**The Pianist** who'd been suspected early in the investigation was performing for another prominent New Orleans family on the day Mr. Kensington died. Her performance was witnessed by many spectators. Therefore, she is not a suspect.

**Cajun Jack, liaison to Mr. Kensington, blacksmith, and former captain of the Onomatopoeia,** was placed in Shreveport, by numerous witnesses, on the day Mr. Kensington died. Although he might have had a motive, Jack is not a suspect.

**Dr. Poirot's Nurse** was arrested, tried, and incarcerated for the murder of Dr. Poirot and the attempted murder of Mrs. Kensington. She cooperated fully with the police and gave a full confession, admitting to her role in the scheme. In her statement, she detailed the conspiracy implicating herself and Dr. Poirot in their attempts to incapacitate Mrs. Kensington, thus impacting her awareness of their search for assets they assumed were hidden somewhere within Kensington Manor. Specifically, she cited the rumored gold fortune as their motive. They intended to blast open the safe. This could only be accomplished with Mrs. Kensington incapacitated or dead. She denied any involvement in the death of Mr. Kensington.

**Frank James, former Confederate soldier, former and founding member of the James-Younger gang, and former member of the Bushwhackers and Quantrill's Raiders,** was alibied and placed in Missouri on the day of Mr. Kensington's passing, with his alibi confirmed by many eyewitnesses. Mr. James was initially considered a suspect, with the motive of revenge, based on the betrayal his gang had suffered at the hands of Mr. Kensington. It was substantiated that Frank James was just one of the many parties seeking the whereabouts of Thorogood Kensington, 'The Bull,' and had visited Kensington Manor on at least one occasion. Mr. James' alibi, however, suggested that he is not a suspect.

**Cole Younger, former Confederate soldier, former and founding member of the James-Younger gang, and former member of the Bushwhackers and Quantrill's Raiders,** was incarcerated at the Minnesota Territorial Prison at Stillwater beginning November 18, 1876, and paroled on July 10, 1901. He is not a suspect.

**Robert Pinkerton, co-director of the Pinkerton National Detective Agency,** and the Pinkerton Agency became suspects early in this murder investigation, based upon knowledge of their visit to Kensington Manor seeking one Thorogood Kensington. The Pinkertons and their agency were later removed as suspects, after providing alibis and evidence suggesting that Mr. Kensington was no longer a target of investigation by their agency, due to lack of evidence against him. His former gang members and co-conspirators refused to incriminate him, honoring their gang allegiance, despite Mr. Kensington's unwillingness to do the same.

**Joseph "Fighting Joe" Wheeler, General in the Army of the Confederate States of America,** was contacted at the time of Mr. Kensington's death and asked to provide a statement on pending charges that may exist against former Confederate Private Thorogood Kensington. In General Wheeler's brief statement, he said, "In light of the current disposition of the C.S.A, and due to lack of evidence, there are no pending charges or active investigations into Thorogood Kensington." Based upon this information, the C.S.A and its Officers are not suspects in the death/murder of Mr. Kensington.

**General of the Union Army of the United States.** This Union General provided this statement with conditions of anonymity. "The Union Army does not have sufficient evidence to prosecute Thorogood Kensington for any crime. Furthermore, Mr. Kensington was pardoned by President Andrew Johnson in 1865 based upon the following oath:"

> *I, Thorogood Kensington, do solemnly swear or affirm, in the presence of Almighty God, that I will, henceforth, faithfully support and defend the Constitution of the United States and the Union of the States, thereunder. And that I will, in like manner, abide by and faithfully support all laws and proclamations which have been made during the existing rebellion with reference to the emancipation of slaves, so help me God.'*

In light of this information, the Union Army of the United States of America, and its officers, are not suspects in Mr. Kensington's death.

## The Accused

**Able Forester, professional lumberjack under contract to harvest lumber from Kensington estate,** was investigated thoroughly to this end. Mr. Forester, a well-spoken individual, provided a verified alibi for his whereabouts on the day of Mr. Kensington's death. When asked about his assistant, he was reluctant to speak on the subject, but ultimately, suggested Mr. Collinsword would fall upon the suspect list of any crime. This had happened in the past, due to his eccentricities, that most people could not comprehend. Mr. Collinsword rarely spoke, preferred to hum softly to himself, and acted in a generally odd way most of the time. The universal misunderstanding of this man and his behaviors made him an outcast everywhere he went. Mr. Forester footnoted his comments by saying;

*'Mr. Collinsword wouldn't hurt a fly.'*

**Mr. Collinsword, assistant logger to Mr. Forester,** was investigated and is definitely a **suspect,** based upon his unwillingness to provide an alibi, and  his unwillingness to discuss his whereabouts on the day of Mr. Kensington's death.

**Marie Louise Jeanne Blanque, Mr. Kensington's half-sister,** has refused to give a statement to the police. The theory here suggests Mrs. Blanque benefited financially from undisclosed sums given to her by Mr. Kensington each month during their visits. The theory also suggests Mr. Kensington had recently made Mrs. Blanque aware that funding to her would stop, based upon Mr. Kensington's financial decline, and based upon Mrs. Kensington's recent knowledge of the Onomatopoeia. Marie Louise Jeanne Blanque is a suspect with revenge as her motive.

## The Suspects

Based upon my deductive reasoning, combined with the case data collected thus far, I have taken the liberty of reducing the active suspect list, in this case, to the following individuals. Further investigation into these two individuals is warranted.

```
           Suspect #1 Mr. Collinsword.
       Suspect #2 Marie Louise Jeanne Blanque.
```

## <u>Case Status;</u>

As I began to delve deeper into the whereabouts, behaviors, and possible motives of these two suspects, my search for clues and incriminating information would ultimately exonerate one of them, thus narrowing my continued focus to just one individual.

This lengthy process was time-consuming and difficult, considering the repeated attempts to affect my removal as envoy to the lady of the house and my removal as chair of the tenancy.

These concerns weighed heavily on my mind and disrupted my ability to perform at one-hundred percent effectiveness. Just as I was about to submit my resignation from my chair position, a surprise gala altered my decision.

```
        Greetings from 113 Rue Cheshire
                  The Kensingtons
    do hereby request your presence at their home
        for a formal gala to begin at 8:00 pm on
            Sunday, December 10th, 1881
------------------------------------------------------------

          ------------------------------
```

The invitation awaited my return to my room, surprising me and piquing my curiosity. Mrs. Kensington had not hostessed a gala in some time, and I wondered about her motives. Was this our final soiree? Was she about to serve us with evictions? At this point, I'd lost my ability to predetermine her motives and actions, and prepared myself both physically and mentally for what may happen. Then, I set out for the grand dining hall on the main floor of Kensington Manor.

ACT 16

# Abel Forester &
# Mr. Collinsword and their
# Bittersweet acquaintance

After further prowling, I mean investigating, in the now abandoned study in the manor house, I came across a lengthy statement given by Abel Forester in support of his assistant Mr. Collinsword. In this statement, Mr. Forester answers numerous questions asked of him by the original investigators. This overly verbose document seems to clarify several sticking points of my investigation. That's my opinion, but I'll let you decide for yourself.

**<u>Statement provided by Abel Forester</u>**

I met Mr. Collinsword in New York state, in the Catskills. To be more specific and to pinpoint the place of our meeting, I'd say Neversink, formerly Bittersweet, NY. I'd have to say that's just what our meeting became—bittersweet. Mr. Collinsword had been alone for many years, at the base of the Catskills, where he'd been abandoned at the age of ten by his birth family when times had gotten too tough. Their whereabouts soon became unknown, and Mr. Collinsword was alone, with no one to keep him company and with no one to whom he could converse. Over time, Mr. Collinsword's desire to speak left him, just as his family had done years earlier. It's not that he cannot speak; it's a matter of not wanting to speak. He will talk in certain circumstances and when forced, but absence of the spoken word is his preferred stance.

I'm not exactly sure of his age, but he was, indeed, a young man upon our first acquaintance. I had descended the mountain for supplies and was in the process of leaving town and returning to my work when I observed this young man on the streets of Bittersweet, or Neversink, whichever you prefer, being ridiculed by several local youths numerous years his junior. Mr. Collinsword did not retaliate, and I wondered if the young man was a deaf-mute. I approached the group and scolded the youngsters for their treatment of Mr. Collinsword, who was obviously in a state of neediness. After assisting Mr. Collinsword, I determined that the verbally abusive youths who had berated him were sorely mistaken regarding their insults and accusations. I found Mr. Collinsword to be quite intelligent, only lacking in the spoken word. For weeks, I just called him Neversink. After all, he was unable or unwilling to provide his name, and he did not seem to mind.

Later, after he'd joined me in the mountains, and after I'd taught him to make fire, cook and clean, and tend camp as necessary, he shared with me his only personal possession. From the hip pocket of his torn trousers, he retrieved a single photo of himself from some years earlier. I could see it was a meaningful keepsake for him. On the back of this photo was the name Collinsword. From that point forward, I have addressed this man as Mr. Collinsword, in an attempt to show him that he is a human being deserving of respect unless his future actions were somehow to suggest otherwise.

Coincidentally, the logging contract that I'd recently acquired mandated that I acquire help. Otherwise, I'd be unable to meet its terms. Upon determining that Mr. Collinsword was energetic and eager, I suggested to him that he begin learning my trade, the trade of lumberjack, and in exchange for his work, he would be paid the standard rate.

Before long, we'd transformed our primitive campsite into a somewhat comfortable and adequately functional base for logging. We constructed a bunkhouse, smokehouse and tool shed, in short order.

Mr. Collinsword took to lumberjacking as quickly and as professionally as any logger I've known, including myself, and soon there was no tree too towering for his swing.

As he continued to excel in his work and as I began to pay him for a job well done, a problem arose, which I addressed promptly.

On the first day of reprovisioning, after Mr. Collinsword had been paid, and we'd already descended the slopes of the Catskills into Neversink, Mr. Collinsword and I separated to attend to our differing personal business.

As I said, Mr. Collinsword, despite his oddity, is quite intelligent, and therefore, it did not occur to me that he lacked the basic concept of understanding money. Don't get me wrong. He fully understands the concept of buying, and that he should pay for the things he wants. He just didn't understand the value of money. This, I soon determined after we'd reunited that day, and all he had to show for a month's pay was a small bag of peppermints.

I took offense right away by confronting the proprietor of the trading post, only to be told that negotiation is not unlawful and that Mr. Collinsword had willingly paid the price being asked.

We did not fell another tree until I'd ensured Mr. Collinsword had learned the ins and outs of money, and that the outs of money occur much easier than the ins.

Before long, Mr. Collinsword became a financial whiz regarding the handling of money. He was never taken advantage of again, at least, in a monetary way.

I never witnessed Mr. Collinsword cry or become angry. I rarely heard him utter a single word. His only vice—the vice that nearly separated us—climaxed on the opposing slope of the mountain, midway through the end of the fulfillment of our contract. I remember vividly that day and what occurred as we prepared to depart.

I declined the assistance offered by my overly eager companion and continued about the task at hand, unassisted. I felt it only proper that I, being the more experienced of the two, should oversee the job through completion. The drudgery which lay before me could, certainly, be finalized more expeditiously in the absence of his distracting vice. Thus, the reason for my refusal. He seemed to take the abatement in stride and continued the low soft humming...

Now, had I a preconceived knowledge of my current disposition, I would have chosen my trade with a more discerning attitude. The immediate job—nothing I would consider optimal for the logger's palette—beckoned my attention, and I obliged. My trusted bucksaw of almost eight years, now seemed hesitant to perform the task, as it swayed to and fro with an awkwardness akin to a drunken stupor. Nevertheless, I proceeded after each uninvited pause and moved closer to the objective at hand.

His humming, having risen now in volume and pitch, aroused my otherwise dedicated senses, and I acknowledged this annoyance with the silent gesture to which he had become accustomed.

He had taken to the profession with indescribable enthusiasm, and I, being a stickler for exquisite work, saw his qualities almost immediately and secured his talent, lest he fall into the hands of my competitor. I often boasted of this business decision, and prided myself, quite deservedly, on having acquired such a fine apprentice. Indeed, I was delighted in his work habits, as they were conducive to my own, and bade him praise regularly. And Mr. Collinsword, being studios in his endeavors, and rarely needing instruction, suited my preferred modus operandi, and we flourished in our chosen profession.

He possessed, however, one trait, one particular idiosyncrasy that, while tolerable when kept in check, was otherwise bothersome and dreaded to my ear. I had, on several occasions, spoken to Mr. Collinsword about the issue, and most recently, issued a reprimand against the violation. Mr. Collinsword's attempts at rehabilitation regarding the aforementioned vice were short-lived, as he always relapsed into the deeply rutted pattern. If not for his impetuous humming, I could have declared Mr. Collinsword's skills as valid and precise as my own. In fact, this particular habit, this annoyance, this piercing continuum, was the only shortcoming possessed by my counterpart.

I arose early the following morning to find Mr. Collinsword preparing for the day ahead. He sat astride the wheel, pumping with enormous ferocity. Sparks showered the wooden floor as he prepped each device for another shift. The sounds of metal to stone, while unattractive, rendered Mr. Collinsword's vice mute. I prepared the bucket lunches for both Mr. Collinsword and myself, and upon completion, moved toward the door. Mr. Collinsword, now having placed a consummate gleam upon the tools, bumped me as we arrived at the door simultaneously. We exited our refuge in concert, fluid in movement as if to know each other's thoughts. We proceeded, as the bird flies, for nine furlongs to the base of the blue mountain. Here, upon the northern slope of the Catskills, we began our day.

Without hesitation, and with much enthusiasm, Mr. Collinsword and I laid full battery to the base of the giant oak. He upon one side and I upon the other, we pulled the willing bucksaw to and fro without resistance. Prosperous sounds filled the air as we felled one after another, in succession. Upon arriving at quota, he, without uttering a single syllable, immediately proceeded to remove each extremity one by one, with most requiring just one swing of the ax. But as he continued to execute each swing with precision, there was never a lull in his vice.

By now, my tolerance for the humming had come to an end, and I really didn't know if his unwillingness to refrain from the distraction was intentional or subconscious. Therefore, I waited until the end of our work day to confront him a second time.

Mr. Collinsword is a fine man, but the humming? I couldn't take it. That's not to say his humming made him a man of lesser quality, but the humming… It became a nearly unbearable distraction.

I've relayed these events to you so that you might be able to grasp the man that is Mr. Collinsword. I suppose your interest in him suggests that he is a suspect in this horrific crime. While I cannot alibi him, and while he cannot be exonerated, at this point, I would recommend that you find someone who has a motive. Mr. Collinsword had no motive to commit murder. He is paid monthly by me, and could not benefit in any way from the death of Mr. Kensington. In fact, I would suggest to you that Mr. Kensington's death had a negative impact on both Mr. Collinsword and myself since our contract was canceled immediately after his passing, as a result of the inquest.

After providing this information Mr. Forester was asked the following direct questions;

## Question #1: Where were you on the day of Mr. Kensington's death?

I left camp the day before Mr. Kensington's death, taking my wagon into town for supplies that Mr. Collinsword and I had depleted during the prior week. Due to the remoteness of our working environment, reprovisioning our camp usually consumed forty-eight hours of my time. During these forty-eight hours, I traveled from our camp to the trading post, where I purchase goods for the camp, for myself, and Mr. Collinsword. I was in New Orleans proper during this entire time, and I can refer you to many witnesses who can corroborate my whereabouts.

## Question #2: Where was Mr. Collinsword on the day of Mr. Kensington's death?

As I mentioned earlier, Mr. Collinsword remained at our base camp, as is our standard protocol during reprovisioning. Mr. Collinsword elects to remain behind, based upon his fear of the public, not to mention, his routine rejection by society. I have found his decision disappointing, but understandable, based upon the abuse inflicted upon Mr. Collinsword during his lifetime. I'd hoped that, over time, Mr. Collinsword would be rehabilitated, considering his employment and his interaction with me on a daily basis. However, his rehabilitation is still a work in process, and progressing at a much slower rate than I'd anticipated. Like I said, Mr. Collinsword was left at our base camp, but I cannot guarantee that he remained there. I value Mr. Collinsword's friendship and hard work. The humming is his only vice, and although I cannot account for Mr. Collinsword's whereabouts on the day of Mr. Kensington's death, I can vouch for his character, despite his eccentricities.

## Question #3 Is it possible for Mr. Collinsword to be questioned with you acting as an interpreter?

Mr. Collinsword does not need an interpreter. He is quite capable of speaking. His silence is a choice. He once told me that the greatest advantage the animal kingdom has over us humans is the inability to speak. I did not understand his comment until witnessing the routine verbal abuse he suffers at the hands of almost everyone he encounters.

**<u>Question #4 If evidence against Mr. Collinsword is discovered and he is tried and found guilty, do you think Mr. Collinsword should be institutionalized or imprisoned?</u>**

Although it is not instantly noticeable, Mr. Collinsword has an innate ability to thrive within any surroundings that he may occupy. With that said, Mr. Collinsword should neither be institutionalized nor imprisoned.

**<u>Question #5 Do you think it's possible that, in your absence, Mr. Collinsword and Mr. Kensington had a confrontation and the ensuing argument enraged Mr. Collinsword to murder?</u>**

I remember the day Mr. Collinsword decided to begin his long tradition of remaining at base camp during reprovisioning. It was in the second year of his apprenticeship with me. We had traveled nearly two days to reach the nearest trading post and general store, and after arriving, we separated, as was our routine, to tend to our individual business. Later that day, I witnessed, from only a block away, a commotion just outside the general store.

Mr. Collinsword had just purchased his peppermints when he encountered a thief in the street. This man not only verbally abused Mr. Collinsword but also struck him. As the man turned to depart with Mr. Collinsword's money, and  Mr. Collinsword's bag of peppermints, the man was knocked to the ground by an errant horse who'd become unhitched from his post. The man's glasses fell from his face and into the street, where they were destroyed underneath the hooves of the horse. It was immediately obvious that this man was heavily dependent upon his spectacles, based upon his behavior just after the incident with the horse. He could not locate the broken glasses, the bag of mints, or the money, even though the items lay in the street, just at his feet. As he began to walk, he extended both arms in front of him, attempting to feel his way forward, much like the blind. Upon taking notice of the man's distress, I witnessed Mr. Collinsword as he walked over to this man, took him by the arm, and engaged in brief conversation with him. Then, I saw Mr. Collinsword lead this man from the street and into the safety of the general store.

Does this sound like a man that becomes 'enraged'?

## <u>Conclusion</u>

I found Mr. Forester's statements compelling, not to the point of exoneration for Mr. Collinsword, but I did believe that Mr. Collinsword was innocent. Therefore, I removed him from my suspect list, so that I could focus on a stronger suspect with the motive for murder.

ACT 17

# Marie Louise Jeanne Blanque

Further investigation into Marie Louise Jeanne Blanque convinced me that she was the most logical suspect. I determined she was most likely to have committed the crime based upon her motive, her unwillingness to talk with police, and her need for money.

Marie Louise Jeanne Blanque, as you already know, may have been Mr. Kensington's half-sister, paternally speaking. The elder Mr. Kensington had more than likely fathered Marie Louise during his secretive affair with Madame Blanque. When Thorogood learned that Marie Louise Jeanne Blanque was probably his sister, he was thrilled. Growing up as an only child, Thorogood had yearned for the closeness and the comradery that he believed siblings could bring to his otherwise lonely life. His loneliness, and his desire for human companionship, only gained in strength throughout his life. He had, in fact, often lost old friends over time, and it appeared he'd lost his wife as well.

Mr. Kensington concealed his secret relationship with his half-sister using the Onomatopoeia as the excuse for his absences from Kensington Manor, and over the years, as Mr. Kensington's emotional dependency upon his sister grew, her financial dependency upon him also increased. After the secrecy of their relationship was uncovered, after her financial dependency upon him was likewise exposed, and after the accounting of his generosity toward his half-sister was summed, the amount was staggering. Mr. Kensington's generosity contradicted his stated desire to maintain the successful operation of Kensington Manor. As a last resort, Mr. Kensington discontinued the financial support for his sister. I believe, in doing so, he may have simultaneously set into motion the events that would lead to his demise.

It was rumored that Marie Louise Jeanne Blanque became enraged after being cut off financially by Mr. Kensington. The messenger who delivered this news to her in person was berated and physically assaulted by Mrs. Blanque. Additionally, rumors swirled about her state of mind as she descended into poverty and alcoholism, with her chosen drink being absinthe. This elixir sometimes referred to as the 'green fairy' because of its color and its psychoactive properties, altered Mrs. Blanque's personality, rendering her delusional, and often incoherent. It wasn't long before her alcoholism was misdiagnosed as mental illness and later, the mental illness misdiagnosed as demon possession.

Her labeling as 'possessed' took place just after one particularly disturbing event that occurred only three months after being disowned and disinherited by her half-brother.

As she sought any and all remedies that might restore the relationship she'd once had with her half-brother, Marie Louise Jeanne Blanque began to visit local soothsayers and Voodooists, believing they could help. During this pursuit of remediation, Mrs. Blanque engaged in ceremonies, rituals, seances, and sacrifices, in attempts to summon some unknown force for advice or assistance. News of these meetings traveled throughout the local parishes and became widely known to the local residents. This news, coupled with Mrs. Blanque's public demonstrations of delusion and incoherency, cemented her labeling as possessed.

It was at a particular ritual that Mrs. Blanque disclosed to the other attendees her intent to kill Mrs. Kensington. Mrs. Blanque had no hesitation venting her intentions to anyone within earshot, based upon her growing disdain and hatred for her half-sister-in-law. It was this singular person whom she held responsible for her financial decline. In her possession that day, she had a large butcher's knife, a dead chicken, a quart jar of chicken's blood, and a Voodoo doll fashioned in the likeness of Mrs. Annie Sue Kensington. That night, down by the river, under the light of a full moon, Marie Louise Jeanne Blanque became particularly demonstrative and appeared to talk in tongues while performing a mock sacrifice using the knife, the chicken, the chicken's blood, and the doll. Later, as many residents witnessed her in the streets of New Orleans they noticed the blood, as it seemed to glow in contrast to her porcelain skin. She regurgitated in the street, and the former contents of her stomach seemed to glow green on the cobblestone. There was no doubt in the minds of those residing in New Orleans that Marie Louise Jeanne Blanque was possessed by Satan.

News of her possession and her hatred for Mrs. Kensington traveled faster than electricity on a wire.

Months passed, and Mrs. Kensington had not died, but what happened next further solidified the notion of her guilt to most individuals familiar with the case.

Vigilantes across New Orleans who feared the Voodooists, and their rituals and sacrifices, gathered outside the home of Marie Louise Jeanne Blanque, calling for her to leave town at once. Mrs. Blanque had not refused to acknowledge their presence but did not hear the gathering crowd, due to her state of inebriation. First, one stone was hurled, and then another, breaking her windows and damaging the exterior of her house, before the crowd was reprimanded and disbanded by the local sheriff.

The next afternoon, as sobriety came to Mrs. Blanque, she exited her home in search of more absinthe to satisfy her addiction. Taking notice of the damage to her home, she fell under the delusion that the evil spirits she'd called upon for help had betrayed her.

This betrayal drove her further into a state of despair, which caused her to drink even more heavily.

That night, after Mrs. Blanque had returned to her home and finished more than her share of absinthe, she attempted to start a fire in her fireplace to combat the cold. These repeated attempts at heating her home failed, driving her into the streets in search of more alcohol of any kind to warm her from the inside. Unbeknownst to her, the final attempt in her fireplace began to flame and the plethora of tinder on the hearth combusted, setting fire to her home. Hours later, upon returning, Marie Louise Jeanne Blanque found her home completely engulfed in flames.

Destitute and homeless, Mrs. Blanque took to the streets, begging for change and strong drink, often spouting about her continued disdain for both Thorogood Kensington and Annie Sue Kensington, often calling out their names in full as she cursed their existence.

Days later, Mr. Kensington would be found dead on the lower level of his manor home. The feathers found on his clothing pointed to multiple suspects, including the young Voodooist who was later exonerated, and Marie Louise Jeanne Blanque.

Authorities began looking at Marie Louise Jeanne Blanque closely, even going as far as arresting her and holding her on multiple unrelated charges while they continued to search for evidence against her. Months later, while Mrs. Blanque remained in jail, the evidence remained lacking, and the now sober Mrs. Blanque was interviewed extensively regarding her public statements about Mr. and Mrs. Kensington, particularly pertaining to Mr. Kensington's death.

The following is the Q & A deposition taken from Marie Louise Jeanne Blanque during her incarceration followed by an additional lengthy statement provided by her.

## Question #1 How do you know Thorogood Kensington?

Thorogood Kensington is my half-brother. We share the same father.

## Question #2 When did your relationship with Thorogood Kensington begin?

I was unaware that I had a brother until Thorogood knocked on my door and began asking all sorts of questions. I'd heard rumors about my mother's affair and about how it caused her and my father to divorce. I never really got to know my biological father. My mother's third husband Leonard Louis Nicolas LaLaurie is the only father I've known.

## Question #3 Have you ever been to Kensington Manor or on the grounds of Kensington Plantation?

Yes. Thorogood invited me to several soirees before we lost touch during the war. I first visited Kensington estate during his sophomore year at Louisiana State Seminary of Learning and Military Academy. I was introduced as a friend so that his father would not know my identity. We thought it best that Thorogood's family did not know my true identity because of our father's scandalous past, so I was passed off as a friend he'd met while away at school.

## Question #4 Have you ever met Mrs. Annie Sue Kensington, and if so, did you have any relationship with her?

Yes. I met Annie at one of the lavish parties held at Kensington Plantation.

I had no relationship with her whatsoever, and she did not know that I was her future husband's half-sister.

## Question #5 Do you know any of the following staff of Kensington Manor, and if so, what is your relationship with them?

- Gweneth Archer - I have never met and did not know Miss Archer. I did hear Thorogood comment that she was an asset to Mrs. Kensington and Kensington Manor.

- Adolfo Carie - I don't know Mr. Carie. Thorogood had described this young man as dependable. That's why I was shocked when Mr. Carie was arrested and relieved when he was found 'not guilty.' It saddens me that he was arrested at all.

- Alphonso Morie - I never met Mr. Morie, but Thorogood spoke very highly of this young man and the way the young man cared for his horse.

- Monks Sterning - My brother never met this fellow and mentioned that there is no one in the employ of Kensington Manor by this name.

- Pearson Brooks - Thorogood often mentioned Mr. Brooks when we discussed his horse. Mr. Brooks kept the animal well shod.

- Cajun Jack - Jack was Thorogood's most trusted employee. Thorogood spoke very highly of Jack, and I understood the two men were close friends.

- Abel Forester - I was aware that Thorogood had contracted a team of loggers to harvest and then sell timber from his plantation. I only heard him mention Mr. Forester on one occasion.

- Mr. Collinsword - I never heard Thorogood mention Mr. Collinsword, other than the one time we talked about his plans for timber harvesting.

## Question #6 Do you know Mrs. Kensington's personal physician and his nurse and if so, what is your relationship with them?

- Condos Poirot - Thorogood did not like Dr. Poirot or his nurse. He felt the two of them were divisive and a bad influence on his wife. He questioned their motives.

## Question #7 What is your current financial/employment status?

I am unemployed and penniless. I depended upon my brother financially, and when his generosity was withdrawn, it affected me negatively and resulted in my homelessness.

## Question #8 Did you kill or conspire to kill Thorogood Kensington, and do you have an alibi for the day he was killed?

No, I didn't kill Thorogood. I was in jail on the day he passed. I'm ashamed to admit this, but I was arrested for public drunkenness and prostitution the day before he died. I wouldn't normally mention this, but I'm well aware that if you investigate me, you'll discover this anyway.

## Question #9 Did you conspire to kill Annie Sue Kensington?

I did not conspire to kill Mrs. Kensington, nor have I ever conspired to kill anyone. I'll admit that I was very angry with both my brother and his wife after being cut off financially, but I'd never kill anyone.

## Question #10 What was your current religious affiliation?

My most recent affiliation is Voodoo. But now, I would consider myself an atheist.

## Question #11 Do you know the whereabouts of the sailing vessel named Onomatopoeia?

Thorogood did, indeed, disclose to me the fate of his schooner. It's at the bottom of the Mississippi River. He scuttled the vessel to prevent our father from using the boat for smuggling and privateering.

## Question #12 Do you have any information on the existence or the whereabouts of Kensington's Gold?

Thorogood always gave me U.S. currency in dollars; it was never in gold. He often talked about his despair regarding his inability to open his safe. He never disclosed to me the contents of the safe, but he implied that something of value was inside. He never hired anyone to crack the safe because he wanted strict confidentiality, and he believed that confidentiality would be compromised if a third party became involved.

## Question #13 Do you have anything to add to your statement that may assist in the arrest of a suspect in this case?

Yes. Thorogood and I became much closer just before his death. He visited me monthly, never faltering in his promise to continue his visitations. During the many visits, we talked in-depth and at length, regarding his Manor home, the staff of Kensington Manor, the operation of the plantation, and his wife Mrs. Kensington.

Thorogood spoke highly of almost everyone on staff at Kensington, with only a few exceptions.

First of all, he disliked Dr. Condos Poirot very much, and he also held the doctor's nurse in low regard. But the bulk of his suspicions were against his wife Mrs. Kensington. Let me read to you this passage from my diary. I transcribed this verbatim, during my last visit with Thorogood, at his request:

"Marie, I need your help. I just don't know what to do. Annie's behavior continues to become odder with each passing day. My suspicions regarding the true nature of her illness are now unbounded. She is hiding something.

The day before yesterday, I went to the basement to have a drink within the privacy of my humidor. When I opened the door, I found Annie inside. She seemed her normal self. By this, I mean, she was addle-minded and appeared lost. I assumed her dementia had gotten the better of her and she'd become lost within the expansiveness of our home. I came to her aid, ushered her from the humidor and onto the lift, and up to the parlor. I left her in the care of her lady-in-waiting, Miss Archer. Something was strange about the entire encounter. As I departed, I accidentally dropped my hat just outside the parlor. As I stooped to retrieve my hat, I could hear Annie's conversation with Miss Archer. The addle-mindedness had gone, and she spoke matter-of-factly and with lucidity.

I'm ashamed to admit it, but the next day, I began to spy on my wife. I noticed her absentmindedness only occurring during my presence, gone entirely when she assumed I was not near. I witnessed her snooping in Dr. Poirot's doctor's bag and decided to test her lucidity at that moment. I entered the room under the ruse of some kitchen matter, catching her in the act. Immediately, her state of mind changed, and she began talking about the doctor's bag as if it were her purse and she was searching its contents for a comb.

Marie, Annie has never carried a purse of any kind. After departing, I waited outside the parlor door, where I overheard Annie ring Miss Archer, subsequently telling her that she should take Dr. Poirot's bag to him because he had forgotten it in the parlor.

The next day, I was approached by my groom. He disclosed to me some unbelievable news and had I not already become suspicious of Annie, I wouldn't have believed him. Alphonso told me that he had been offered a large sum of money if he would assist my wife in stealing my palomino. When I asked him why he had no further details. By this point, I assumed the horse would be sold after it had been 'stolen,' and the proceeds would be used to pay my groom, with the remainder left for the principals involved. I suspected Dr. Poirot had had a hand in this premeditated theft. That's when I decided to sell her myself. I thought removing the temptation would diffuse the situation. Afterward, my closest friend and confidant, Jack, approached me with yet more unbelievable news. It's based upon this news, Marie, that I must ask you for a favor...

I think my wife is trying to kill me. If something dreadful befalls me, can you relay what I've told you to the authorities?"

## Question #14 Why did you not inform the authorities about Mr. Kensington's disclosure and request immediately after his death?

I was upset with him for cutting me off financially. It was only later that I learned he'd made accommodations for me in his last will and testament.

I haven't finished reading this entry from my diary to you; my brother goes on by saying:

"Jack told me that Mrs. Kensington's footman, Mr. Monks Sterning, was hired as a patsy. They intended for him to take the fall for my murder, if the authorities discovered that I had, indeed, been murdered. Jack also told me that he had witnessed Annie's 'selective' memory, as he called it, and that he was sure she was faking her memory loss.

After hearing this latest news, I decided to approach Mr. Sterning with the threat of arrest in exchange for his confession. What I learned about him solidified my suspicions of my wife. As I moved about Kensington Manor, and as I interviewed the staff, I could not locate one individual who'd met Mr. Sterning. No one there could describe him or his features, leading me to the conclusion that this man did not exist. I also discovered that a 'Monks Sterning' was listed routinely within the payroll ledger of Kensington Manor, being paid monthly, just like other staff members. Further investigation revealed that this 'Monks Sterning' was fabricated and used for embezzlement of the Kensington Manor payroll. The sad part of this, I believe, is that Annie learned how to steal from a payroll from the many stories I told her about my past. I, basically, gave her step-by-step instructions on the subject.

I decided to confront her about all of this, but before I could, I caught her, again, inside my humidor. The day this happened, I went to have a drink in the humidor. Before opening the door, I peered through the small circular window. Inside, I saw my wife snooping around in search of something. I placed my ear to the door, ever so carefully, and listened. I could hear her muttering to herself. Barely discernible, I overheard the words 'combination' and 'safe.' Repeatedly. There was no mistaking it; she assumed I'd hidden the combination for the safe somewhere within the humidor. I also heard her mumbling, 'If I don't kill that Rhino, somebody else will.' This is the phrase inscribed on my safari mount. I asked myself, 'Why would she be reciting those words?' Then it became crystal clear to me. I'm the Rhino."

## Question #15 Do you believe Mrs. Kensington killed her husband, your brother?

Yes.

# THE FINAL SOIREE?

I was first to arrive in the hall, where I noticed right away, the place settings were already arranged, but not in the order I'd expected. My normal place, just beside Mrs. Kensington, was occupied by the dish normally reserved for Beauregard. Right away, this sight made my hair stand on end and my heart fluttered with anxiety. Maybe his attempts at discrediting me had finally taken hold. Moments later, I could hear the sounds of my approaching housemates from somewhere down the corridor. One by one, they each filed into the dining hall, taking their usual places at the table, with the exception of Beauregard. He took the spot nearest the place where Mrs. Kensington normally sat. I just stood there, refusing to accept my demotion, until I'd heard it straight from my hostess.

Beauregard said nothing to me during the time we waited on Mrs. Kensington's arrival, but I could tell by the smirk on his face, he had gained some sort of advantage over me. He looked like 'the cat that swallowed the canary,' as they say. His guilty satisfaction was clearly imprinted on his face, and I'm sure my housemates noticed.

Mrs. Kensington entered the room and began serving all of us, just like she'd done in the past. After taking her place, she informed us of the new developments regarding our future tenancy. As I'd anticipated, all of us were being asked to vacate Kensington Manor. All of us, with just one exception. Beauregard had been selected as the one who was now indispensable. I couldn't believe my ears. He'd finally swayed Mrs. Kensington to his way of thinking. I was surprised, upset, and heartbroken. She cited lack of funding as the reason for our pending evictions, but by now, I believed there was a more sinister ulterior motive.

As you know, my ongoing investigation had alibied or exonerated all previous suspects, ultimately elevating a new suspect to the top of the list. Mrs. Kensington was now the primary suspect in Mr. Kensington's death, and I believe she was aware of my progress into her involvement in this crime, and the evictions were nothing more than her way of preventing her exposure. And even though all of the clues pointed to Mrs. Kensington, my investigation was still lacking in evidentiary material.

The statement provided by Mrs. Blanque would be considered hearsay in court. It may have been seen differently, had the information been in Mr. Kensington's hand, but that was not the case, thus rendering the document hearsay. At best, the only evidence against Mrs. Kensington would point to her guilt for embezzlement, but the party responsible for filing charges would be Kensington Manor and its management. Now that Mrs. Kensington held sole ownership of Kensington Manor, charges would not be filed, and further investigation would not be pursued. She'd gotten away with it; Mrs. Kensington had planned and executed the perfect murder in killing her husband Mr. Thorogood Kensington. I probably should have been anxious to leave. I mean, who wants to live with a murderer? On the other hand, she was always kind and generous with her boarders. In a way, I wanted to prove to myself that she was innocent, even though the evidence was, frankly, difficult to dispute.

After the main course, we were each given an additional treat, our last meal, you might say, before being forced out. But rather than being served by Mrs. Kensington, these treats were given to us by a middle-aged woman I'd never seen. She entered the room, summoned there after Mrs. Kensington jingled the bell that she'd retrieved from her apron pocket. The woman carried a silver tray, upon which sat Mrs. Kensington's tea and our treats. She placed the tray on the table, served the tea to Mrs. Kensington, then dispersed the nine treats, one by one. All of us were silently surprised, except for the newly-appointed envoy of Kensington Manor. He swallowed the treat without chewing, making a spectacle of himself as he ate. I would not learn the woman's identity until the next day when I overheard Mrs. Kensington conversing with an old acquaintance by telephone.

"Yes, that's correct. She started a few months ago," Mrs. Kensington said. "Miss Archer is here as a live-in. She was employed by Kensington Manor years ago and comes to me from Standingford House, where she managed the entire staff for years. Her knowledge of budgeting will certainly help me to get my house in order. I'd like to resume deliveries to my home, and I'd like to introduce you to her. Are you available for tea tomorrow evening around six? That's wonderful news. I look forward to seeing you again."

The next evening, Mr. Bainbridge failed to arrive at six. His appointment with Mrs. Kensington had been canceled just moments after being arranged, and would not be rescheduled. Miss Archer had plans for Kensington Manor, and Mr. Bainbridge did not fit into those plans. Mrs. Kensington remained unaware of the cancellation and assumed Mr. Bainbridge had reconsidered the continuation of deliveries.

At ten minutes after six, a dialogue initiated by the newest and only employee of Kensington Manor, Miss Gwen Archer, began as follows.

"Mrs. Kensington, I'm afraid Kensington Manor has developed a reputation no longer suitable for the status and prestige it once knew. I'm unable to hire anyone qualified to assist in the restoration and operations of your home. As you can clearly see, common delivery men are unwilling to work for Kensington Manor. I'm afraid an indelible black spot has been made on your manor home. And, after reviewing your finances, I've learned that there is a substantial sum of back taxes owed. At this time, I advise you to sell your estate."

Mrs. Kensington did not seem surprised by the news regarding the condition of her estate, but she was surprised at the frankness used by Miss Archer to convey the news.

"And, that subject that you've delayed for months? We need to address that now. I know this will be a difficult decision for you, Mrs. Kensington, but it's time. It's time you find them new homes."

"Can't I have at least one of them stay behind? I've grown so fond of them all."

"One, maybe, but nine? Your finances will no longer support them."

Now, it all made perfect sense to me; Beauregard wanted to be the 'One.'

After months of resisting and delaying the inevitable, Mrs. Kensington reluctantly agreed to the liquidation of her estate, including her manor home and us, her boarders.

I took this information, that I'd acquired through eavesdropping, back to my housemates, placed it before them in committee, and waited for the vote. It was too late. Beauregard's influence had won them over. My motion was defeated, with one in favor and eight against. Even Pandora saw no hope any longer, opting to vote with the other dissidents. I was devastated.

My motion had been a simple one. I suggested that we return to those days of old, those days when the galas were lively and carefree, by resurrecting and catering a gala in honor of Mrs. Kensington. After all, it was quite possible that her abrupt discontinuance of our residency might be reversed if the correct tactics were implemented. And maybe our efforts in showing our appreciation to the lady of the house would be rewarded in kind, with extended lease agreements, which in turn, would restore the house to the state of normalcy it had once known.

I will admit that this method of entrapment, based upon the tugging of Mrs. Kensington's heartstrings at the party to be held in her honor, may seem somewhat insincere. But we, that is, my housemates and I were out of options and had consumed the full length of our rope. My housemates' disagreement with me was evident by their votes.

Beauregard recorded the results in the ledger, then made a motion to close, after setting the date for each of our forthcoming departures.

The following week, we met again to iron out the wrinkles in our plans to vacate Kensington Manor.

The eight of us just sat there, waiting for Ginger to arrive. It was not like her to be late, so, we continued waiting. Once Pandora realized the reason for the delay, she made us aware of Ginger's disposition. Apparently, Ginger was the first of us to leave. She had found a new and welcoming environment in the French Quarter, and as they say, when one door closes another door opens. So Ginger exited our house with the door closing behind her and entered the door held open for her in the Quarter, leaving the remaining eight of us there to plan our futures.

Mr. and Mrs. O'Keefe were next and informed us of their imminent departure from Kensington Manor, scheduled for just after our meeting. Their former plan, to create vacancies at Mrs. Kensington's home, had never come to fruition. At least, not in a way beneficial to them. It had also damaged their relationship with their close friends, the ones to whom they'd promised residency. This damage resulted in their isolation and a reduction in sympathetic companions locally speaking, so they decided not only to leave Kensington Manor but also to leave New Orleans. They planned to return to St. Louis.

You would think Beauregard would have been happy with this progress, but that was not the case. And even though all the others appeared on the roster ahead of me, he skipped all of them, focusing his attention on me, and demanding to know why I hadn't left with the O'Keefes.

That's when Josephine interrupted by making us all aware of her plans. It appeared that she'd been up all night and crying. She looked disheveled, and it was obvious her eviction was taking a toll on her. She did not want to return to her former abode, due to an undisclosed reason, and therefore, agreed to meet the O'Keefes later to see if she could join them in hopping a train bound for St. Louis.

The very next morning, both Kitty and Rose departed Kensington Manor without disclosure of their plans or their destinations. I assumed they were returning to Alabama. I made this assumption based upon their mutual states of homesickness, which both of them had exuded, but never mentioned outright. This left only three of us behind awaiting eviction from the manor house.

Beauregard, Pandora, and I had no additional meetings regarding our tenancy or regarding Mrs. Kensington and Kensington Manor. By now, it was just assumed by a certain individual that he'd be the sole survivor of this mass displacement, but that result had yet to be established. I still had some ideas on resolving this amicably, with that result too, yet to be established. Regardless, the showdown between the two of us was imminent.

The next few weeks were odd, in that I rarely interacted with the others, even though our paths did cross occasionally. I'd notice Pandora's flirtatious behavior, now being shown toward the both of us. Maybe it was because she was hedging her bets on which one of us would prevail. I'm not sure. Anyway, I continued to think about launching one final attempt on securing long-term housing for the remainder of us. Kensington Manor was more than large enough, and I could see it working out. I still believed that Mrs.

Kensington would have allowed us to stay, if not for the insistence of Miss Archer.

Pandora was the next one of us to depart. I hadn't expected her abrupt retreat from the house, considering her most recent amorous interest in me. Nevertheless, she left that day, insinuating that she was done with both Beauregard and me and could, ultimately, do better. My relationship with her was one of those paradoxes that we sometimes encounter during our lifetimes.

The latest departure left just me and him there, envoy and former envoy, last-to-arrive versus first-to-arrive, and as I delved deeper into my memory, I couldn't recall Mrs. Kensington ever voicing a preference toward him. Could it be that I'd been had? Outsmarted by this charlatan? Maybe he had just switched places with me and had somehow convinced me that the switch was sanctioned by the lady of the house. That was it, I realized, he'd employed a clever ruse against me, and his appointment as envoy had never taken place. Once he'd secured the affections of a majority of the other housemates, he'd executed the precisely-planned psychological coup. If I'd been the hat-wearing kind, I'd certainly have tipped my hat to him. It was brilliant. I'd been the mouse to his cat in the game we both played.

After determining I'd been tricked, I decided to play a game of my own. The advantage would now be Jasper Peabody. You see, he knew that he'd tricked me, and I knew that he'd tricked me, but he did not know that I knew that he'd tricked me. This one aspect of the game gave me the upper hand. So, I always say, one ruse deserves another, and just knowing what was about to happen placed an ever-widening smile upon my face. If it was psycholog-ical warfare he wanted, it was psychological warfare he would get.

Since Mrs. Kensington no longer called the shots at Kensington Manor, I decided to implement my retaliation upon Miss Archer. So, for the next two weeks, I followed Miss Archer and committed her schedule to my memory, including her meal times, tea times, and nap times. It seemed to me that her daily life was rigid, prompt, and never wavering. Even the time she spent with Mrs. Kensington was scheduled, as if by appointment.

While watching Miss Archer, I noticed that she departed her room promptly at 2 p.m. each day, just after her afternoon nap, and did not return until 8 p.m., just after serving Mrs. Kensington's evening tea. I also noticed that she routinely left her door ajar upon exiting and that, as she walked the corridor toward the staircase, she often said 'Hello' to Beauregard as they passed one another within close proximity. These weak points within their routine schedules would be attacked first.

The next day, at approximately 7:15 p.m., I heard a scream originating from Miss Archer's room. The blood-curdling yell was so intense, it made my hair stand on end. Next, I heard Miss Archer yelling at the top of her lungs, "BEAUREGARD!"

Next, I saw him—the charlatan—running wildly away from her corridor, where he slept each evening, and down the stairs.

I attempted the charade the very next day, with very similar results.

"BEAUREGARD!" I heard Miss Archer yell, followed by him scurrying away.

My third attempt, however, failed. As I approached Miss Archer's room with the dead rodent, I found her door closed, preventing me from placing the fresh carcass on her pillow. It was time to change strategies.

The next day, I approached Miss Archer's closed door at 2:15 p.m. sharp. From just outside, there in the corridor, I commenced issuing numerous cat-calls near her keyhole, in an attempt to disturb her nap. It worked just as I'd planned.

No sooner had I turned the corner at the end of the corridor, than an angry Miss Archer exited her room and swung a newspaper at the 'guilty' party as he cat-napped in the hallway chair.

One day later, I entered Miss Archer's private bath, where I unspooled the entirety of her toilet paper from the spindle and onto the floor.

Once again, Beauregard was blamed. It was now time for the knockout punch.

I was not usually one to impose such a distasteful strategy on an opponent, but as they say, all's fair in love and war. Well, this was not a matter of love, but it was definitely a matter of war, and I have to admit, his initial victory over me had damaged my ego. So what happened next, while vile and disgusting, was necessary for bringing this war to an end.

Later that night, after going to bed, and somewhere in the early morning hour of 2 a.m., I awoke to take my nightly trip outdoors. Instead, I went straight away to Miss Archer's door, where I found it wide open. This wide-open-door policy had been implemented so that Miss Archer could hear, in the event Mrs. Kensington were to call out to her during the night. So, without hesitation, I entered Miss Archer's room and defecated on her silken sheets, just near the foot of her bed. I did all this with a stealthily and silent precision often used during offensive strikes in wartime.

I woke the next day to find myself as the only remaining boarder at Kensington Manor.

In consideration of our dislike for one another, and despite my covert operation against him, I would have gladly called a truce, had he only been honest with me. Sometimes, war forces us to do things that we'd otherwise not consider. I'd much rather have taken the route of peace, And, had that peace plan moved forward, this is how the invitation would have read;

```
        Greetings from 113 Rue Cheshire
              The Kensingtons
   do hereby request your presence at their home
     for a formal gala to begin at 8:00 pm on
          Sunday, December 10th, 1881
-----------------------------------------------------
          ---------------------------------
```

## ACT 19

# THE CONFESSION

I laid low for several weeks following Beauregard's eviction. I felt it better to employ the out-of-sight, out-of-mind strategy, at least until I could figure out what I should do next.

To make this happen, I became more nocturnal, choosing to take care of my business during the nighttime hours and choosing to sleep during the day. That's when I began to notice that Mrs. Kensington had resumed her late-night conversations with her late husband.

Seeing the light underneath her door, I approached and listened like I'd done many times before. From what I could gather, it appeared that Mrs. Kensington was engaging her husband in conversation while lobbying for his forgiveness.

Night after night, she pleaded with Mr. Kensington to release her from the guilt she carried with her for her deception of him regarding her sickness, and for the guilt she felt over his poisoning. She also begged him to understand that she'd acted in haste, due to his deception regarding his half-sister and the Onomatopoeia, and regarding his ability to hurt so many people while only showing remorse when he felt threatened with capture. These unanswered pleas commenced each night with her refrain only on Sundays.

I'd learned during my prior snoopings that Miss Archer kept a diary of her dealings and experiences at Kensington Manor and that she wrote in this diary nightly. The time of this chronicling coincided with Mr. and Mrs. Kensington's late-night conversations. I thought this coincidence was too good an opportunity to pass over.

The next night, I waited in the corridor for the light beneath Mrs. Kensington's door to illuminate. Once I received this signal, I moved straight away to Miss Archer's room and peeked inside through her open door. She sat at her desk writing in her journal, just as expected. What I did next was done solely to entice Miss Archer to Mrs. Kensington's door. So, without hesitation, I darted into Miss Archer's room and swiped her favorite pen, once she'd laid it down upon her desktop.

"Mr. Peabody?" she blurted out in a whisper. "What are you doing?"

Well, you already know what I was doing, but Miss Archer did not. So, I ran from her room, going only fast enough to prevent my capture, while slowly enough to ensure she did not lose sight of me, carrying her pen the entire way. During the pursuit, she continued to call out to me in a whisper. I suppose the faint voice was her attempt to avoid waking Mrs. Kensington. Then, just as we approached Mrs. Kensington's room, I dropped the pen in the light that glowed underneath her door and darted away.

Miss Archer bent and retrieved her pen, then noticed the light coming from the lamp inside Mrs. Kensington's room. Just as she was about to knock, she heard the ongoing conversation from inside. Humans are funny this way, in that, they only have to be enticed once when the prize is a wealth of knowledge obtained through eavesdropping.

The next night, I watched from the end of the corridor as Miss Archer waited for Mrs. Kensington to light her lamp. Then with, diary and pen in hand, Miss Archer approached Mrs. Kensington's door, where she listened and transcribed.

This went on night after night for the following three weeks before I noticed a change in their patternistic behavior, prompted by an inquisitive Mrs. Kensington.

"Gwen, dear, you look tired. Why, you can hardly keep your eyes open," Mrs. Kensington said as Miss Archer served her evening tea.

"Yes, Ma'am, I've had difficulty sleeping," Gwen replied.

"Is there something troubling you?" Mrs. Kensington asked.

By this time, I'd determined that the real Mrs. Kensington was not at all like the Mrs. Kensington that most everyone thought they knew. And I worried that she'd coerce Miss Archer into incriminating herself regarding her eavesdropping and her nightly recordings. Something—a gut feeling, I suppose—suggested to me that Mrs. Kensington was aware she'd been discovered by her only employee.

The next night, Miss Archer did not come to Mrs. Kensington's door. I imagine she stayed away, fearing she'd been compromised. I returned to my room, hoping Miss Archer would return to Mrs. Kensington's door the following night, but she did not. So, I made a rash decision I believed would break the case wide open.

Just after the light from Mrs. Kensington's room became visible, I approached her door, deliberately bumping it forcefully enough so that I could be certain Mrs. Kensington had heard. Immediately, her door swung open wide revealing where I sat in the corridor just outside her room.

"Mr. Peabody. Where have you been? I'm delighted to see you," Mrs. Kensington said to me affectionately. "So it's you who's been at my door each night."

I neither confirmed nor denied her allegation, but I was certain that my ruse had insulated Miss Archer from any further suspicion. I spent about ten minutes in her room before leaving her alone there, in deep conversation with Mr. Kensington.

The next night I pulled the old favorite-pen-routine, luring Miss Archer to Mrs. Kensington's door, where she resumed her nightly recordings of Mrs. Kensington.

Two weeks later, I overheard the following telephone conversation initiated by Miss Archer.

"Yes, that's correct. We would like to resume deliveries at once. Can you be here at 9 p.m. tonight? Yes, I understand that is an unusual time, but you'll understand why once you've reviewed our purchase order. I needn't remind you, this is a sizable account… Wonderful, I'll see you tomorrow night at nine."

The next night, after tea time and after Mrs. Kensington had retired to her room, just as the clock struck nine, Mr. Bainbridge arrived at the door of Kensington Manor. He was eager to discuss the reintroduction of his contracted delivery services to the large manor home. Miss Archer greeted him and suggested they meet within the seclusion of the lower floor so that Mr. Bainbridge could obtain a current inventory count for the staples stored there.

"Mr. Bainbridge," Miss Archer began nervously. "I'm afraid you've been deceived. I've called you here under misleading circumstances."

"I'm afraid I don't understand," Mr. Bainbridge replied as he evaluated the vegetable storage bins.

"Please read this," Miss Archer said as she handed her diary to him.

"What's this?" Mr. Bainbridge asked.

"Please read, Mr. Bainbridge. I'm afraid we may be compromised if you stay here much longer. Start with this passage," Miss Archer explained as she pointed to an entry in her diary.

Mr. Bainbridge began reading, turning page after page, eyes widening and fear overcoming his face. Then, after reading approximately fifteen pages, he stopped abruptly and said, "You can't be serious."

"But I am, Mr. Bainbridge, I recorded those words verbatim."

"Why are you telling me these things?" Mr. Bainbridge asked.

"I've heard that you were a policeman before retiring and starting your delivery service. Is that true?"

"Yes, that's true, but I hardly see how that relates to Mrs. Kensington."

"Can't you take this to your precinct and have them investigate?"

"My retirement was many years ago. All of my former comrades have retired or moved on. I hardly think they would take this seriously. Also, if I remember correctly, Mr. Kensington's death was meticulously investigated at the time, and there was never enough evidence to convict anyone. I think your diary would be viewed as nothing more than the ramblings of a senile old lady."

"But, what if it's true? It sounds like a complete confession to me."

Mr. Bainbridge remained silent for an extended time as he continued to thumb through Miss Archer's diary.

"I don't see how I can help," he finally admitted.

Then Mr. Bainbridge turned hastily and climbed the stairs, with Miss Archer only steps behind, pleading for his assistance. As the two of them turned the corner at the top landing and entered the kitchen, they were startled to find Mrs. Kensington there in her wheelchair, wide awake.

"You didn't tell me we were having company, Miss Archer," Mrs. Kensington said.

"Is everything okay, Mrs. Kensington? It's unusual to see you up and about at this hour."

Mrs. Kensington did not reply. She simply stared at the two of them.

"Mr. Bainbridge is here to provide us with an estimate of valuation on your remaining inventory, isn't that right, Mr. Bainbridge?"

"Uh, yes, yes, it is. I'll get those numbers back to you as soon as possible,"

Mr. Bainbridge replied nervously before attempting to depart Kensington Manor.

"Won't you stay for tea?" Mrs. Kensington asked as she followed behind him to the manor door.

"No, thank you, Mrs. Kensington. Not at this late hour."

"Mr. Bainbridge?" Mrs. Kensington began. "How is it that it is too late for tea, but not too late for business estimates?"

Just as both Miss Archer's and Mr. Bainbridge's fears were nearing their climax of being caught red-handed, Mrs. Kensington voiced her allegations against them.

"Tell me, Mr. Bainbridge, does your wife know about Miss Archer?"

This accusation nearly made both Miss Archer and Mr. Bainbridge burst out with laughter, but they fought the urge.

"No, she doesn't," Mr. Bainbridge replied.

"I hardly think your wife will believe you're sailing at this late hour," Mrs. Kensington sneered.

"No ma'am, I mean, yes, ma'am…. I'll get back to you with those estimates soon. You ladies have a good evening."

After Mr. Bainbridge had departed, Mrs. Kensington began to scold her employee on the nature of virtue. Miss Archer accepted the scolding without disputing the allegations of Mr. Bainbridge's infidelity and left it at that.

"Sorry to disturb you, Mrs. Kensington. Good night," Miss Archer replied.

Three days later, Mr. Bainbridge agreed to meet with Miss Archer in the park to review her diary once more.

I stood behind a nearby tree and watched as she waited on the bench in the park for him. Her movements indicated that she was beginning to worry that he'd changed his mind about their meeting and her diary. Miss Archer was, by this time, an emotional wreck, constantly looking over her shoulder, expecting some unknown and awful fate to befall her. Mrs. Kensington had been generous and kind to her, but after overhearing the confessions and suspecting Mrs. Kensington knew about her diary, Miss Archer felt she'd been left with little choice.

On the one hand, she did not want to leave Kensington Manor and the lifestyle that working for Mrs. Kensington afforded her.

On the other hand, safety was now preeminent. If Mrs. Kensington had the wherewithal to poison her own husband, then what was her limit? Was Mrs. Kensington actually capable of killing again?

Mr. Bainbridge arrived while Miss Archer was deep in thought, and his presence, while not sudden or unexpected, startled her as she had not noticed his approach. The two of them sat on the bench for the next hour-and-a-half, reviewing the many hand-written entries in the diary.

The overwhelming evidence against Mrs. Kensington suggested to Mr. Bainbridge that Mr. Kensington had, indeed, been poisoned by his wife and that her motive was a simple one. She felt deep resentment over the betrayal and the disrespect laid upon her shoulders by her husband. His actions toward her implied he felt no love for her whatsoever, and his financial improprieties ulti-mately sealed his fate.

Mr. Bainbridge reluctantly agreed to take possession of the diary and to convey his suspicion and the diary's contents to the authorities at the precinct where he was formerly employed.

Miss Archer thanked him, departed, and made her way back to Kensington Manor, looking behind periodically as she walked, to ensure that she'd not been followed.

An entire month would elapse before Miss Archer saw any result based upon her meeting with Mr. Bainbridge. *The wheels of justice move slowly*, as they say, and Miss Archer's nervousness became increasingly visible to Mrs. Kensington upon each subsequent interaction between them. Unfortunately, the result Miss Archer had expected was not the result that Miss Archer received.

On the thirty-second day after their meeting in the park, Miss Archer and Mr. Bainbrige reunited to discuss the result of the reopened investigation into Mr. Kensington's death. Miss Archer's diary was returned to her, along with the following explanation.

While the evidence was strong against Mrs. Kensington, it was still circumstantial and, possibly, hearsay. Mrs. Kensington had not confessed to any authority, and any good lawyer would argue that Miss Archer had fabricated the contents of the diary in retaliation against her employer.

She argued her point with Mr. Bainbridge and made numerous emotional pleas for Mrs. Kensington's arrest. However, that event would not be forthcoming. The local authorities had declined any further criminal action in the case, citing a lack of evidence.

Miss Archer found herself in a compromised position. Should she seek new employment, or should she remain at Kensington Manor? She asked herself these questions repeatedly after leaving the park.

She did not sleep very well that night, and her lack of sleep was beginning to affect her work. Mrs. Kensington noticed the recent change in Miss Archer's overall demeanor and countenance, which fueled elevated scrutiny of her work habits.

Then, just as Miss Archer was at her wit's end, an unexpected phone call soothed her nervousness and restored her confidence.

"Kensington Manor, Gwen Archer speaking. How may I help you?"

"Miss Archer?"

"Yes, this is Miss Archer. How may I help you?"

"This is Gordon Bainbridge."

The sudden silence on the telephone line suggested to Mr. Bainbridge that Miss Archer had disconnected the call.

"Miss Archer, are you there?"

"Yes. Yes, I'm here," Miss Archer replied after clearing her throat.

"I have some interesting news for you regarding the case. Can we meet?"

"Yes," Miss Archer replied.

"Same location, noon tomorrow," Mr. Bainbridge said before hanging up the phone abruptly.

The next day, Miss Archer sat on the same bench where she'd sat during her previous meetings with Mr. Bainbridge. She ate her sack lunch and waited patiently for him to arrive.

During their brief meeting, Miss Archer was informed of a pending motion to exhume Mr. Kensington. She welcomed the news with tears, crying all the way home to Kensington Manor.

ACT 20

# THE EXHUMATION OF
# THOROGOOD

Holt Cemetery, a potter's field, was opened for business in 1879. This burial ground for indigents did not seem like an appropriate choice for the interment of a man like Mr. Kensington. But after Mrs. Kensington refused to pay any of his funeral expenses, the city of New Orleans had little choice. Mr. Kensington was laid to rest in Holt Cemetery ten days after his passing. In the years afterward, he remained there in his subterranean resting place, undisturbed until the following happenstance.

In 1935, the Times-Picayune published an op-ed piece entitled "Schrodinger's Gold." This article, written by a young reporter attempting to make a name for himself, was based upon the unsolved murder of Thorogood Kensington. The writer combined the mysterious circumstances regarding the murder with the newly published theories in quantum mechanics of Erwin Schrodinger and his barbaric and unnecessary science experiment, 'Schrodinger's Cat'. Much like  this unfortunate cat, who had been closed within a sealed box, so too, had Kensington's Gold. Schrodinger's experiment involved a vial of poison similar to the rumored accusations regarding Mr. Kensington's demise. During the experiment, the cat was exposed to poison. However, the time of death for the cat could not be pinpointed, since the poisoning occurred within the privacy of the box. Mr. Kensington's death was similar in this regard, as well. Based upon Schrodinger's experiment, a question arose. When does supposition end and reality begin? In other words, is the cat alive, or is the cat dead? The possibility of imagining the cat alive is real, but so is the possibility of imagining the cat as dead. After so many years of mystery, the question of Schrodinger's Gold was born. Did Mr. Kensington possess a fortune in gold at the time of his death, or did he not possess a fortune in gold at the time of his death?

Not even a week had passed after the publishing of this article before an attempt to exhume Mr. Kensington occurred. His grave at Holt cemetery became the target of grave robbers known to frequent the easily accessible burial sites of New Orleans. Rumors regarding the gold suggested that Mr. Kensington took it with him. Oddly enough, this notion that he'd been buried with the gold was enough to spur the thieves onward in an attempt to exhume his body and steal his fortune.

Luckily, a beat cop patrolling between City Park Avenue and Rosedale Drive that night overheard a disturbance from within the closed cemetery. The unorganized and greedy pair of thieves argued about the methodology and workload of the exhumation, and this resulted in their arrest. The next day, in an effort, to prevent further scavenging, the Times-Picayune published a follow-up. The newspaper falsely reported that the thieves had been successful in exhuming the body, but no gold had been found. This ruse halted any further attempts to unofficially exhume Mr. Kensington.

Months later, based upon the confession within Miss Archer's diary, an official exhumation of Mr. Kensington was ordered by the coroner of Orleans Parish. Again the Times-Picayune published a series of articles chronicling the event for the residents of New Orleans.

Coincidentally, it was during this time that many advances had taken place in forensic science, particularly pertaining to the detection of poisons within cadavers.

Six weeks after Mr. Kensington's official exhumation, the coroner's report was delivered to the District Attorney of Orleans Parish and to Gordon Bainbridges' former police precinct. No gold had been found, but Mr. Kensington had, indeed, been poisoned. The levels of arsenic within his body were staggering. And although arsenic had been introduced into his body during embalming, it had not been introduced in such massive volumes detected by the coroner.

The District Attorney decided this new evidence warranted another interview with Mrs. Kensington. Miss Archer was notified by telephone of the results of the autopsy and the imminent visit from detectives.

The next morning, a tremendous pounding summoned Mrs. Kensington to her Manor door. All that she said after flinging the door open wide and seeing Gordon Bainbridge there, along with two uniformed officers was, "Thorogood! Where have you been?"

ACT 21

# INSINCERELY, MR. PEABODY

After Mr. Kensington's exhumation and the subsequent determination that he'd died from poisoning, Mrs. Kensington became the primary suspect. There was a wealth of hearsay that pointed at Mrs. Kensington, but there was also circumstantial evidence that pointed to multiple other suspects. These facts created a reasonable doubt about any one person's guilt. No one had witnessed Mr. Kensington's poisoning directly. It was proven that he had ingested the poison from the tainted whiskey bottle within his humidor. How the contents became tainted was the unanswered question. Mrs. Kensington, Cajun Jack, and Alphonso Morie, all had access to Mr. Kensington's humidor. Also, the whiskey may have been poisoned before arriving in the humidor, which opened susceptibility to nearly the entire staff of Kensington Manor. Many still suspected Mr. Collinsword of the crime. Suspicions also revolved around the young Voodooist, despite his acquittal. This reasonable doubt boded well for whoever had poisoned Mr. Kensington.

Just after the murder, the remaining staff had resigned, choosing to leave Kensington Manor over fear for their safety, or in pursuit of better pay. Years later, feeling terribly lonely, Mrs. Kensington resorted to the boarding of us strangers. The rehiring of her former lady-in-waiting, Gwen Archer, was a last-ditch effort to save Kensington Manor.

Unfortunately, since the cat had not gotten Mrs. Kensington's tongue, and because the non-profit nature of the boarding venture had depleted her already drained resources, Kensington Manor was shuttered. Mrs. Kensington's designation as senile and unfit to prosecute forced her to seek an assisted living arrangement. I remember the day they took her away. She removed a cameo locket from the chain around her neck and attached the locket to my collar. Then she drew me close and whispered in my ear, "Take care of yourself, Mr. Peabody."

## Where are they now?

As you already know, all of the boarders, with the exception of yours truly, left Mrs. Kensington's manor home in pursuit of other interests. I kept in touch with some of them, and some of them, I did not. Below is an accounting of their current dispositions as relayed to me, directly or indirectly, via third parties:

**Josephine** remained in New Orleans. I suppose she had second thoughts about accompanying the O'Keefes to St. Louis. I saw her several times as I strolled the Quarter, looking like something the cat dragged in. I felt sorry for her in one way and indifferent in another.

**Kitty & Rose,** the sisters from Alabama, returned to their home state. I hear the move took a toll on their relationship and their mental health, now they're just cats in the cradle.

**Mr. & Mrs. O'Keefe,** I never saw again. I suppose they're now living somewhere in St. Louis. And while I never really had anything against his mate, Percy O'Keefe isn't even fit for cat-gut.

**Beauregard,** as you know, was the last to be evicted from Kensington Manor. Some small part of me still expects him to show up seeking revenge, like a bad penny or a cat with nine lives, never really going away. The way he strutted about makes it hard for me to accept that he would just slink away, especially once he realized my role in his expulsion. All I can say about him is, '*The guilt of my dark deed disturbed me but little.*'

**Ginger** landed on her feet. I hear she is gainfully employed at a local dive on the Rue Bourbon. It's my understanding she does her turns on the catwalk there for tips, and room and board. I'm happy to hear she found her calling outside the walls of Kensington Manor.

**Pandora** continues to play a cat and mouse game with me. She's made no secret of her affection toward me, but I'm no mouse. To surrender to her would be akin to defeat, and I'm not ready for a relationship like that. I'm a cool cat, a soloist, a solitary feline. I cannot comprehend a relationship with her or any other kitten.

As for me, **Mr. Jasper Peabody**, former envoy and current solitary resident of Kensington Manor… I'm not exactly a fat cat, but if you were to ask how I'm doing, and if you could see me now, you'd know by my **Cheshire grin**.


## Conclusion


You may be asking yourself: *What was Mr. Peabody's true interest in solving this case? What was his motive? Did he suspect Mrs. Kensington all along? Why did he relentlessly pursue a suspect and a resolution?*

Let's just say, my interest was self-serving. I did not suspect Mrs. Kensington until I learned about the entries in Marie Louise Jeanne Blanque's diary, transcribed verbatim as dictated by her paternal half-brother Thorogood Kensington. This essentially let the cat out of the bag.

Initially, my goal was to exonerate Mrs. Kensington, thereby ensuring my continued residency in her manor home, preventing me from being reduced to an alley-cat. I'd never been treated so well. I felt like a real cool cat living under her roof, an all-around cat's meow, if you will. If it hadn't been for that copycat, Beauregard, wanting my job and causing such a disruption in the house, then maybe the others wouldn't have been evicted. I've been told he's now a cat burglar, stealing just to survive. I can't say I'm surprised.

Sometimes an investigation can yield answers to questions that we now regret asking. It can also lead to loss of life.

However, in this case, curiosity did not kill the cat. Still, it did get eight of them evicted, leaving one former fat cat alone, where he now fends for himself within the expansiveness of the recently condemned Kensington Manor.

So now, without further adieu, I will consider this investigation closed. Thank you for tagging along.

inSincerely yours,

Jasper Peabody.

*P.S. - And the Gold?*

That's right; I almost forgot. To date, the safe behind the portrait that hangs on the wall above the mantle in the grand dining hall of Kensington Manor has not been opened. Therefore, the gold may or may not be inside. I really can't say one way or the other. That's why it's still known as *Schrodinger's Gold.*

# CHARACTER INDEX